Waters of the River

SUSANE LAVALLAIS BOYKINS

SUN RED BOOKS LLC

Paperback: ISBN-13:978-0998522104 (Sun Red Books LLC)
              ISBN-10:0998522104
Hardcover: ISBN-13:978-0-9985221-1-1

Printed in the United States of America.

Library of Congress Control Number: 2016920571

DEDICATION

For David Wendell, Chantelle and Lisa

ACKNOWLEDGMENTS

I'd like to thank my son, David Wendell Boykins, for his unending support and advice.

I'd like to thank Huey L. Perry, Ph.D. and Donald G. Prier Sr., Ph.D. for taking the time to preview and critique my work, as well as, give me encouragement.

I'd like to thank the Greater Fort Worth Writers group for their assistance in helping me get a good start.

I'd like to thank Cole Lavalais for her advice about the art of writing.

CHAPTER 1

Marksville, Louisiana, August 1960

What is the meaning of my life? What real thing do I have to show for the sacrifices I have made? These thoughts permeated my being to the point that was unbearable. Tears filled my eyes and I could barely see. I heard the mournful wails of her grieving mother and the youthful hollers of her inconsolable child. Through the blurriness of my tears was the outline of my childhood friend's anguished husband, as the arms of his brothers held him back from throwing himself upon her casket as it was being lowered into the earth. An awful wail filled the air and I knew it came from him.

"Ashes to ashes, dust to dust," said the pastor. My own resolve began to slip away and I began to sob uncontrollably. Arms encircled my waistline.

"Aaw Ma chére, she fine now. She in a bett'r place. Wouldn't come back yuh fur nothin'," she whispered in my ear, in her strong creole accent. I closed my eyes and turned away from the scene and felt such a pain in my heart that I wished I would faint to get some relief. I nodded my head up and down in understanding. From the center of my being, I summed up the strength to get my emotions under control, so the pain in my chest could ease. I wasn't sure Keykey would not want to come back to her husband and child, but it was not something I wanted to argue with my mother about at such a moment. Besides that, our faith taught me that she was now at peace.

"Mom, I need to go." I knew I needed to leave to keep my sanity.

"All right, Bay. Ah know it bees hard on ya. And it so hot out yuh. We kin go if ya wan'."

My mother only called me "Bay" at times when she consoled me. As a child, after I would hurt myself, she eased the pain with a kiss or a rub and would call me "Bay". It helped me to relax. As we walked back to our car, arm in arm, we passed by graves old and new. The southern sun beat down upon us and I felt a slight breeze flowing through the pecan trees that lined the side of the fence that bordered the graveyard and the church. In my mind, I could still hear the choir singing the old hymn, "In the Sweet Bye and Bye" from when we went to the graveyard. That song always brought forth feelings of heartache. I remembered as a child, I would stand outside of the church house doors at funerals, and watch family members of the deceased as they filed by the casket in different stages of grief. I would weep incessantly as they wept, because I felt their pain. Now, I was the one who was grief-stricken. Now, I was the one overwhelmed by my sorrow. As my eyes surveyed the landscape, the familiarity of the white wood framed church, the open meadows and the occasional house that dotted the rural neighborhood did not make me feel any better. Tears of sorrow rolled down my cheeks as we left the cemetery and drove home.

Kesandra Richardson, whom everyone called Keykey, had been my comrade in arms for as long as I could remember. We first played together at the age of five. On that day so long ago, we played hide and seek in the green grass and bushes of her parent's front yard. We did not unglue ourselves from each other until she'd gotten married and I had gone away to college.

When she died peacefully in her husband's arms, after a long bout with cancer, our bond was broken forever. Keykey told me often that she and her husband, Blaine, always slept intertwined. She could not sleep if she did not lay her head on his chest and feel the beat of his heart. I told her that when I had suggested the same thing to my ex-boyfriend, he'd told me it was too uncomfortable to sleep that way. He'd said nobody could sleep like that. I could hear her voice now, "Oh Char, not my Blaine. From Day One, I have slept on his chest. I know it is selfish of me. But I can't sleep without it, and he let me do it. He's never pushed me away one time because he was uncomfortable. Ain't that something? He let me." She would then smile and get a far away look in her eyes, nod her head and say, "That's my man and God knows I love him."

She'd been so lucky to be adored like that. I closed my eyes and tried to imagine how it must feel to be cherished in that manner.

I realized if I passed away today, I did not have the same feeling of contentment. The goals I'd achieved had satisfied me to a point, but there was still a void deep within my soul. My body had not produced and nurtured another being. No one curled up with me at night and allowed me to feel the warmth of their body.

I felt empty inside as I faced life without her friendship, and envious because unlike her, I felt unfulfilled in my quests for a consequential life.

That had to change. I didn't know how I would change it. Something was missing and I needed to find out what it was.

CHAPTER 2

I prayed to myself: Lord, help me get through today. I felt the familiar heaviness in my chest that had been a constant companion since the death of my best friend. But I have a new school year to start and I have to stay focused. I can't grieve today.

As I rushed down the small graveled lane where I lived and then the blacktopped road, I remembered the time my grandfather's tractor slipped into the deep ditch at this turn. At six years old, getting the tractor out of the ditch seemed an insurmountable feat. Then like magic, people appeared from the different houses as far as my eyes could see. I was astonished at how fast everyone, both black and white, came together communally to strategize and execute the safe retrieval of our tractor. The following weekend, we'd waved at some of our white neighbors in town, and they passed us by or looked over our heads or in other directions, but never at us. Just like they didn't know who we were.

That's the way it was down here. Everyone pulled together in times of crisis, or for work, since most of the Black farmers sharecropped. The races did not socialize otherwise.

As I drove down the road, I thought of Keykey. It had been two weeks and I really missed her. I swear, she knew what I was going to say before I said it. We could talk without words.

My heart still yearned to hear her voice. I'd taken long walks on the plush green levee, which framed the Mighty Red River. The levee protected us from the river's wrath during hurricane seasons, when its banks overflowed with the clay colored water. I had sat on its apex and looked into the calm, yet still moving murky waters and found a haven to meditate and contemplate the loss of Keykey and the direction of my own life. Just like the moving current of the river, with its twists and turns, is not deterred by logs, broken limbs and debris, I could not be hindered by a broken heart. I had to start a new year of school, although it's the last thing in the world that I wanted to do.

Teaching elementary school had been the fuel that sustained my life. I remembered, as a child, when I sat in class and watched how teachers smiled when students entered the classroom or answered questions, or patted a child on the head or shoulder to make them feel better after being bullied by another child and I'd thought, that's what I want to be, a teacher. My family was poor, so at the time, there was no way I imagined going to college, but I'd done it. I'd felt proud of that. But now, the vacant feeling in my soul, made me aware that I needed more than teaching in my life. That insight sent a shock wave through my system that clouded my perspective.

I was alone on the road except for an occasional car or tractor. The green pastures were sparsely littered with cattle and fields were ablaze with the South's white gold, cotton. People, some of them my age, most of them friends and relatives, dressed in cover-alls and straw hats, pulled long sacks over their shoulders that dragged behind them. They had labored since the break of day. I knew they would be there through the harsh midday sun until an hour or so before sundown.

Gratitude and empathy filled my heart, because there, but for the grace of God go I.

As I rushed onto the campus of the all-black school, my feet hurt. I cursed under my breath and admonished myself for not breaking my new shoes in. Flat shoes had been my footwear of choice all summer long, except for church on Sundays. This had not prepared me for the rigors of walking around in high heels all day. All around me were throngs of people, different shapes and sizes.

Several students ran up to me. "Hi Mrs. Ford," they said in a chorus. They grinned widely as they pushed and shoved each other to get my attention.

"Hi," I said. "Calm down."

One of the children said, as he jumped up and down in front of me, "Miss Ford, Miss Ford, can I bring Toby to school one day? Can I? Please, can I?"

"Toby, who's Toby?"

"My dog, Ms. Ford. Can I bring my dog one day, like they did in your class last year?"

I laughed out loud. I remembered the trouble I had gotten into with my principal and my students' parents last year, because of my "Bring Your Pet to School" project.

"I don't know about that," I laughed. I knew I would not do that again this year, but I didn't want to get into it right then. "We will see." I walked briskly to the entrance of the school.

When I reached for the door handle, I saw a large masculine hand with long fingers and felt the softness that comes from not working in the fields as it closed over mine. "I got it," he said.

"Oh, Mr. Dean. I didn't see you coming. Thank you." I stepped back and let him open the door for me.

His eyes looked piercingly into mine and his lips spread into a warm smile. My heart quickened.

Control yourself, I told myself. He is striking, but he is

married.

"You're welcome, Miss. Ford." Then the smile left his face and his eyes. "Look here, I couldn't help but hear those students ask you about pets. Now, you do know you can't do that again, right?"

"Yes, I know." My face grew hot and I nodded my head as I recalled how I'd tried to reason with my principal. "Mr. Pearson was livid. He stood toe to toe with me and told me he felt like firing me and I believe he really meant it."

He touched my arm and slightly turned me toward him, to get my full attention. "He did. He did really mean it," he emphasized. "I admire your originality. That was, definitely, a different kind of student motivation, but impractical. Don't try him again. My brother-in-law doesn't play."

"I know and thanks for the advice."

Mr. Pearson had reprimanded other teachers, but never me. I'd always received excellent evaluations and praises for different projects I'd done with the students.

We reached the beginning of my wing, and his clean-shaven, medium brown complexioned face changed from brows drawn up tight into a pleasant smile. "We have after school bus duty together this week. I'm looking forward to it."

"You are looking forward to bus duty?" I asked. "You are kidding?"

"Well, I'm looking forward to spending time with you."

My eyes studied his face to see if he was flirting with me. His smile seemed innocent enough. "Okay, see you then."

I watched his strong well-built frame walk away in his crisp white shirt, black tie and slacks. That feeling of excitement invaded my chest. Indeed, he was a very appealing man and I reminded myself to not let my loneliness play with my emotions. He was a married man, thus unavailable.

As I walked to my classroom, I heard my heels click on the

concrete floor of hallways that would soon burst with black children. These school buildings were only four years old. This was thanks to the Brown Vs. The Board of Education of Topeka case of 1954 that ruled, "separate educational facilities are inherently unequal." So, the Avoyelles Parish School Board, in an effort to prove them wrong, decided to build a new black school, so they could say, "See it's separate and equal." Of course, it still wasn't. The white school was bigger with more amenities, such as bigger labs, libraries, etc. But this was much better than the outside toilets, Baptist Church, store front and other makeshift buildings we'd had before. Thus, I felt good as I walked down the hall. The rough textured beige cinder block walls were fresh from their summer scrubbing and were clear of any marks or graffiti.

I silently prayed for a good beginning and attempted to bring back the excitement I usually felt on the first day of school. Keykey's death made this all seem pointless.

My classroom was at the end of the hall on the east wing so there was no way to avoid Mrs. Delores Batiste as she approached me. I liked her well enough. I just did not feel like talking to her today. Her face was serious and her eyes were sad. "Miss. Ford, I was so sorry to hear about Keykey. I know you two were close."

With the mention of Keykey, I felt the tears that were just below the surface begin to peek out and make their presence known. I dabbed my eyes and I heard my voice quiver, "Thank you, Mrs. Batiste. It's been tough, but I think school starting will help me. It will keep my mind busy."

"Yeah, you're probably right. How's her family doing?"

"Mom has been going by there and bringing food. I go too, but not as much as she does. It's just so hard to see them." I looked toward my classroom door. I wanted to make a quick exit. To change the subject. "I love that suit. It is new, isn't it?"

I walked to my door. Before she could answer, I disappeared inside.

The bell rang, and the students rushed down the hallways.

By the end of the day, I was exhausted. There was, however, one more chore to do, the very necessary stint of bus duty. My students who rode buses followed me out to the boarding area.

Memories of other bus duty stints passed through my mind. How about when my teeth chattered from the cold? How about when I sweated bullets in the heat? Suffice it to say, this was not one of my favorite extra duties. Because with teaching, there were always extra duties.

I took a deep breath and attempted to drive my exhaustion out of my mind as I noticed seven buses lined up. Their large yellow bodies reminded me of yonder days when I rode similar buses when I was in high school. Before that I'd walked to school, sometimes four miles one-way.

These kids are so lucky and they don't even know it, I thought.

I spotted Mr. Dean, who was already there.

"Hey, Miss Ford. See you made it." He flashed that magnificent smile.

"Did I have a choice? I don't think I have a choice," I answered and smiled.

"Well, let's get started. I'll take the first three and you take the last three and we share the fourth."

"That sounds fine to me," I said.

To oversee kids after a long day, whose energy is still high as they look for ways to expel their pent-up vigor is a feat that requires concentration and patience. In one of the lines I handled, two different groups of students argued with each other.

"Emily, what's going on?" I said.

"Miss Ford, they keep making fun of my skirt," she cried. "I'm sick of it. She say she gonna hit me. And if she do, I'm gonna beat her."

"Oh no, you're not and she is not going to hit you, either," I proclaimed.

There were three girls in Emily's group and five youngsters in Peggy's group. I turned toward the other group and said, "Peggy, what's going on?"

"Nothin', Miss Ford. I dunno what's wrong with that gull. She always messin' with people."

Right about the same time, I saw a crowd of kids separate and form a circle. Loud voices screamed and cursed each other, and the onlooker kids yelled and shouted and provoked the conflict to continue. In the middle of the crowd, arms flew about and I heard licks hit their mark. My heart beat faster, because this was happening in one of my other lines.

I wondered how I was going to handle two situations, a girls' argument and a boys' fight?

Mr. Dean stepped over to where the boys were fighting and without hesitation injected his body as fists flailed about. At least one landed on his jaw before he separated them. He never flinched. Wow, I thought, he took that punch and never batted an eye.

The boys stood on both sides of Mr. Dean. The crowd continued to holler to motivate the two boys to resume their fight. I left the girls as they argued and situated myself where I could see the individual faces of the instigators. Once they knew I could see who they were and they were no longer anonymous, they quieted down. "Cut it out now. It's over. Whatever it was, it's over now. You all hear me?" he said.

With the crowd quiet and the realization that they would go to the principal's office in the morning, their young bodies relaxed.

He stood between them and said, "Fighting does not solve anything. When you're finished fighting, the problem is still there. Talk about it. There's a good chance you'll solve it."

"I just don't like him, Mr. Dean," said one of the boys. The other nodded his head in agreement.

"Then stay away from each other." he said sternly.

My two little girls groups I'd dealt with had become interested in the boy's fight, and forgot about what they'd fought about. With the fight resolved, everyone boarded their bus.

I handled most of my discipline problems. I very seldom sent anyone to the principal's office. However, I was truly grateful he'd stepped in, because I usually supervised smaller kids and I didn't want to step between almost-grown fighting boys. I don't think I could have taken the blow he'd taken.

"Thank you very much," I said. "Are you alright?"

"You are very welcome. He got me pretty good, but I'll live," he said, with a nervous laugh.

"Do you want me to go get you some ice or something?"

"No, I'm okay. Really."

"Well, I'm glad you were here. It's good to have friends who can handle themselves in all types of situations."

"I don't know about the handling myself in all types of situations, but you can always count on me to do whatever it is that I can do," he said.

Being impressed by someone does not come easy for me. Still, in spite of the way Mr. Dean had been hit, he remained composed and in control of the situation. This gave me a new appreciation of him.

"Since most of the students are gone now and we are out of earshot of the ones still here, do you mind if I call you Charlotte?"

His request took me by surprise, but I thought about it and decided that I didn't have a problem with it. Teachers address each other as Mr. or Miss in the presence of students. It forms a barrier of distinction and respect between the students and the teachers. "You can call me Charlotte. May I call you Ray?"

"Ray sounds perfect," he smiled.

"Ray, you are very much respected here by the students and the teachers. After today, I see why?"

"Well thank you, Charlotte. Experience. Patience. Empathy. To name a few of the things I have learned over the years to help me in this job."

"Over the years, you're not that old to be using terms like 'over the years'," I said.

"I'm thirty-five. How old are you?" he asked.

Feeling defensive for some reason, I'd said, "I'm twenty-five, and proud of it."

"What's a girl like you doing in a place like this?"

I laughed. "Why am I a teacher? Is that what you're asking?"

"Yes." His eyes sparkled.

"I have always wanted to be a teacher. Teachers are respected leaders in all parts of life in the black community. They lead in school and church. What other kind of a profession can a black person have? You're a preacher, teacher or undertaker. I worked hard to become a teacher. It was a hard road, and it always seemed so far away."

"What's wrong? Why are you sounding sad about it? You are a good teacher. You made it."

"Watching a child when they finally get something you have been trying to show them is an exceptional feeling. It makes you feel like you're doing something worthwhile. But, lately I have been wondering why I was so fixated on accomplishing that particular goal and not so much on some others."

Why am I doing this? Why am I pouring my heart out to this man? I wondered.

He looked at me thoughtfully, as if he had read my mind, and said, "Why is a tall beautiful woman like you not married? I know the men at Grambling College are not crazy. So how in the world did anyone not snatch you up?"

"Who says somebody didn't?"

He slowly let his eyes drift to my hands. Self-consciously, I covered my left hand with my right hand. I knew he was looking for some kind of ring, wedding, engagement, or friendship. None was there.

"I don't want to talk about it," I said.

He put both his hands up, as if to defend himself. "Okay, I'm sorry for getting too personal. But I see something in your eyes and face that I think you need to talk about. That you want to talk about. I'm a good listener."

"I'm fine. Really. I don't need to talk."

I exhaled and relief flooded my soul as the last busload of children began their ride home.

"Well, it's time to go. Thanks again for corralling those boys. It's a shame all of the good men are taken," I said, immediately sorry I had said it.

His eyebrows shot up in surprise and then his face, despite the redness from the wallop he'd sustained, broke into a tremendous smile. It totally intoxicated me. "Well, thank you. I think that was a compliment."

"It was," I said. "I didn't mean anything by it." I felt very self-conscious and uneasy and I busied myself by piddling in my purse.

He sensed my nervousness and said, "It's ok. Don't sweat it. I understand what you meant. Didn't take it to mean anything more. I just need to get hit in the jaw more. If that's what it takes to be appreciated."

We both laughed and the tension in the air eased.

"Charlotte, I would say we need to stop meeting like this, but because of the demands of our job, I will see you tomorrow at the same time, same station".

"Sounds like a plan to me. See you tomorrow," I agreed.

CHAPTER 3

I turned into Dr. Frank's neighborhood and passed well-manicured lawns, with pecan trees, magnolia trees, rose bushes, multi-colored flower beds and fences lined with pine trees. Even though the country air was fresh everywhere in this country town, somehow, it still seemed to be fresher here. In some ways, it was like I'd stepped into a different world.

It was four-twenty five p.m. when I reached Dr. Frank's house and my mother got off work at four-thirty p.m. So I parked in front and waited. She had been Dr. Frank's maid and worked in his big fine mansion since I was a child.

Dr. Franks' house stood majestically back from the road. Great columns graced the front, suggestive of a plantation home. I remembered at thirteen years of age, being asked by my mother to deliver dinner to Mrs. Frank one Christmas Day. Evidently, a deal had been struck between the two of them that since Dr. Frank was out of town and their children weren't going to be home for various reasons, my mom could have Christmas off, if she provided Mrs. Frank with dinner. I had been commandeered to deliver the meal, driven there by a cousin of mine. Mom brought home the utensils and other items necessary to complete her agreed upon duty. I was in awe of how the tray had been set up with different plates, plate covers, silver ware and napkins. It was complete with a small shiny silver vase that displayed a single rose. My instructions were to go to the back door and knock. When Mrs. Frank, a slim well-dressed white lady answered the door, I stood there transfixed and starred at her and at the décor of the kitchen, with my mouth opened. Her eyes opened wide and her lips expanded into a wide smile, as she uncovered each dish on the tray. "My, my, my. What a delightful tray. It looks delicious," she said.

I mumbled, "Mom sent this to you." I handed her the tray, and scurried back to the car. I thought, she must be going somewhere dressed like that. With makeup and stockings. We never dressed up unless we were going somewhere, or maybe it's because she's rich and we're not. That's the conclusion I'd come to. And the kitchen was almost as large as our whole house with lots of cabinets painted a light yellow.

Ray Dean's face and smile found its way into my mind. I wondered what he was doing right now. I smiled to myself, and some of the day's tensions eased from my body.

There weren't any eligible single men left in Marksville. When I'd finished college and came home to live, the men in my age range had left town or married. My boyfriend from high school had died in Vietnam. It looked like my future lay in being an old maid schoolteacher. I'd come to accept that. But now I wanted a chance to experience some of the joys of having a family like Keykey.

Dr. Frank's front door opened and a short, medium brown skinned, attractive, middle aged woman in a maid's uniform, walked across the huge lawn. Love and pride entered my heart as I gazed upon my mother, Josephine Ford. Most people called her Feen. She walked with her head held high, hair neatly tucked in a bun, shoulders back with a brisk gait that did not betray how tired I knew she was.

"Been waitin' long Charlawt?" said Mom, in her thick creole accent as she entered my car.

"Just got here. Mom, I'm tired," I said and pulled away from the side of the road. "I have over thirty-one kids and after school duty all this week."

"Girl, what you talkin' bout tied. You dunno what tied is. Walking round dressed up all day," she answered. "Hmm." She chuckled.

My face tightened and I bit down on my teeth hard in an effort to not express a sarcastic retort.

I waited a moment, and allowed myself a chance to regroup. Then I said, in as nice a voice as I could muster, "Mom, you wear heels on Sunday and you can't wait to take them off when we get home. Think about wearing them all day long. Besides, just cause I'm dressed up doesn't mean I'm not working hard. Do you think I just skip off to work, suck my thumbs all day?"

"You ain't pulling no sack of cotton in the hot sun or haulin' no big pot off a stove or on ya knees scrubbin' no flow," she said looking at me with a smirk on her lips as if to say "Gotcha."

"No, but I'm still working hard," I explained patiently, still in a syrupy voice. "I am physically exhausted from standing and walking in heels all day and mentally drained from dealing with kids." I shook my head in exasperation. "I know you know about kids, Mom."

"Yeah, Ah know 'bout kids. Ah sho' do, but dat a whole lot better'n what Ah jes said."

Hopelessness inundated me. How could she understand? Her life was so different from mine. She'd had to quit school in the third grade to go work in cotton fields and private homes to help support her siblings.

We rode for a while in silence, "Sometimes it's so hard to talk to you."

"Chile, didn't ya haf thirty one chil'ren last yer? It work out, didn't it?" She paused and looked at me.

So you did hear me after all, I said to myself.

Then a little more softly, "So, keep ya head up. 'Ah kin do all things through Christ who stren'hens me'," she said.

"Yes, I know. Last year, I ended up with twenty-eight, which is a number that I can handle." I knew she did not really understand my plight. She simply was trying to placate me. But she had always been there for me and I could not forget that. I remembered the time the white man my daddy sharecropped for showed up at the bus stop when I was going to school. I was about nine or ten. He walked up and his belly hung over his belt, already sweaty and it was only about seven o'clock in the morning. I could hear him breath. He wanted to know where I thought I was going? There was cotton in the fields to pick. School wouldn't do me no good, no how, he'd said. I'd stood transfixed, not knowing what to say and feeling very much intimidated. Mom had not left for work yet and stepped onto the porch. She tilted her head to the side, put her hand on her hips and told him in a firm voice "Leave 'er alone. She gwan ta school taday. Ah cut my day short taday at Mrs. Frank and work 'n de fields. I kin pick much as 'er 'n de time Ah gits back til supper den she do all day." He grunted, got in his truck and drove off. I was so proud of her that day. Mom did not want us to be like her. She wanted us to have an education.

"Dat's right. It will be okay. If you jes keep doin' the best ya can do, everythin' will be all right. Whatcha want for supper?" My mother asked, invading my thoughts.

Before I answered, I saw a flash of light sparkling from a shiny surface in the distance. It was a red and white Chevrolet parked in front of our graying unpainted house.

"Mom, it's Adrian."

Her eyes lit up, she laughed. "Lawd, haf mercy, he got a new car."

Through the side of my eye, I saw her as she smoothed her hair back. "What you primping for? It's just Adrian," I said.

"Not primpin'. Jes' wanta be presentabl', s'all."

Adrian leaned nonchalantly against his car. He was a tall slender light skinned man, what some people called "high yeller." He approached my car as we drove up.

"My God, where y'all been? I've been here since 'bout four."

"Boy, ya know Ah don' git off til four thirty," my mother said lightheartedly. "Why you wait out yuh? Angie's inside."

"Yeah, I know," he said as he helped my mother out of the car and leaned down and kissed her lightly on the cheek. "It's cooler out here under this old pecan tree." He said as he pointed at the tree in front of our small-unpainted house. In an effort to add some light to the otherwise dismal view, my mother had planted gardenia bushes in front of the porch on each side of the steps, and the strong fragrance was overpowering. "Thought I would take y'all for a ride in my new car and then get something to eat?" I circled the car and he planted a light kiss on my cheek.

"You a life saver. Cuz Ah am real tied. Monday, my roughest day. Ridin' in a new car and no cookin' sound wonderful."

"Oooh, that thing sure sparkles," I said. I rubbed my hand along the side of the car and admired the chrome, red interior and fin-like back fenders. "What is it?"

"1960 Chevrolet Bel Air," he said, with his chest puffed out.

"Angie," my mother called. "Come on out yuh." When Angie didn't come to the door, "Let me go see what she doin'."

As my mother went into the house to find my little sister, Adrian's eyes fell directly on me for the first time, since we arrived home.

For a moment, we stood and smiled at each other. "Haven't seen you since last year."

"Thought it was time for a visit. Needed to check on Mom and Dad. And I needed to give my car a run on the highway. You know, kind of blow her out. You looking better and better, little girl."

"I am five feet eleven inches. I am not little," I laughed. "You must have me mixed up with my mother."

His eyes twinkled, "Aw, you mean, because you're taller than she is. You're both beautiful women."

A rush of heat engulfed me and I found it difficult to continue to look into his hazel eyes. "Well, I'm grown now, with a job and everything."

"So, I guess you're telling me I can't ride you on my back anymore," he teased.

My mother and Angie joined us.

"That's a pretty car," Angie said. "Hi Adrian. You going to teach me how to drive?"

Everyone said, "Drive?"

"Well, Char won't teach me and Mom doesn't have a car, so that leaves you," she said as she poked Adrian in the chest, with a big grin and with the innocence of a twelve year old.

"You are not ready to drive, young lady," he said. "But when you are, I'll handle it one way or another. Don't worry about it."

Gratitude filled my consciousness at his words. Adrian had always stood in the gap for Daddy. Ever since he'd left twelve years ago.

"Let's go by Joe's Bar-B-Q shack," I said as everyone got into the car and the new car smell filled my senses.

"How long you going to be here?"

"Headed back to Houston on Wednesday. Just a turn 'round trip to see my folks."

"Is ya married yet?" Mom asked.

"Feen, I knew I would not get away from here without you asking me that. No, I'm not married."

22

"Jes' checking," Mom said. "I got ta know wha's happ'ning, as the youn' folks say."

"Yeah, right."

"Adrian, have you heard from Daddy?" I asked. All activity in the car stopped, followed by deafening silence.

Adrian continued to drive as if he hadn't heard me. "Adrian, when did you talk with Daddy last?"

He fiddled with his collar and said, "You are just like your mom. She wants to know if I'm married and you want to know if I talked with your father. No, I have not talked to Lucien. I haven't talked to him in 'bout twelve years, since 'fore the last time you talked with him."

"I just don't understand, how he could leave us and not come back," I said.

"Charlawt, Ah done tol' ya, Adrian dunno where Luke is. Why ya keep axing 'bout him and puttin' ya self through dat? Huh?"

"I don't remember Daddy. I wish I could," Angie piped up with her lips poked out.

"Angie, you know I told you that you were a baby when he left," I said.

"Dat's right, Angie," said Mom. "Y'all Daddy a good man. Dunno why he up and gone. Dun prayed on it and he gonna come back one day. Jes' wait and see. He'll haf a good reason why he lef'." More softly, "Bay, leave it alone. We happy right now. Leave it be."

"I'm sorry, everybody," I said. "Sorry for opening up old wounds. I just still worry about him."

"Dat's okay, my baby. Let's enjoy Adrian. He would tell us if'n he knew," Mom said.

A few minutes later, we drove up in front of a small wood framed red building with a huge wood white sign that read Joe's Bar-B-Q painted in red letters. When Mom and Angie went inside, Adrian pulled me aside. "Charlotte, it looks like you need to talk.

You seem down. I'll pick you up tomorrow and you can talk 'bout Luke all you want without upsetting your momma and Angie."

I reached up and hugged him around his neck. "How do you always know what I need? You are so special to me."

His hazel eyes gleamed as he grinned and said, "That's because you're my chocolate princess."

I smiled and kissed him on the cheek and I remembered the first time he'd called me that. He hadn't called me that in a long time. Any more discussion concerning my daddy would have to wait until tomorrow.

∞

Adrian drove up outside of my house in his red and white Chevrolet. I ran out to meet him. He said, "Let's go for a walk down by the river."

"Ok. That sounds good."

As we walked the familiar path, I felt the peace that entered my soul whenever I embarked on this journey to the river. The dirt road had a few gravels on it to service the few trucks that ventured this far down this lane. Adrian leaned over and picked up a few rocks and began to toss them in the bushes beside the road.

"Your Mom and Angie okay?"

"Yeah, they're fine," I said. "Angie is doing homework and Mom is shelling peas."

"So, what's going on with you, Charlotte?"

"Do you remember Keykey, Kesandra Richardson, Blain's wife?"

He looked at me with a blank stare and then awareness crept in. "Yeah, know Blain. His wife younger than me. Mom told me she died."

"Yes, she did and I guess I need someone to talk to. I always talked things out with her. And now she's gone and I don't know where Daddy is."

"Oh, that cute li'l girl with the big plats you used to play with all the time? That's Blaine's wife?"

"Yeah, that's her."

"I 'member her. I'm sorry 'bout your friend, but what does one thing have to do with another?"

"I'm not sure. I just have this restless feeling I can't seem to shake and it all seemed to be connected to Keykey and Daddy. Keykey is gone and she's not coming back. Because of that, I feel as though I have to solve the mystery of Daddy."

Wind blew through the trees, which lined each side of the road and gave a small degree of coolness to a hot August day. He took my arm as we climbed the green-carpeted levee.

"Lucien was a good man. But, I don't know where he is. My gut tells me he is okay."

"You were good friends with him, even though you're about ten years younger than him. And then when he left, you continued to come by and see us. You even gave Mom money when we needed it. In fact, you sent me money when I was in college. Boy, let me tell you, it usually came at the right time."

He looked into the red muddy waters of the river and said, "Well, Lucien and I were good friends." He looked at his hands and then over the horizon. Then continued, "It's a long story how we became friends. Maybe one day I'll tell you about it. But, I just felt so bad about the way he left and all." He continued to look away from me and then began to shake his head in disbelief. "Feen is such a hardworking woman, but I knew even with all the hard work she did, she'd still need help. So, I tried to give her a hand whenever I could, Charlotte, whenever I could."

"And I'd like to thank you for that." I put my hand on his sleeve and he looked down at me.

"No thanks necessary. I get at least one good home cooked

meal from her every time I come and all the news, because she knows everything that goes on. But gettin' back to you feeling restless, I understand what you mean. I have to admit that I feel that way sometimes."

"You do? Why do you think that is?"

"Well, with me, I feel a void. Not for the same reasons as you, obviously, but a sort of impatience, none the less. But, I think you do know what you're feeling. I think it's because you lost two very important people in your life. People you counted on. And you know why one's gone and you would like to know what happened to the other one. I wish I could help you with that, but I can't."

"So, what kind of void do you have and why did you say you feel that way?"

"I didn't say, young lady, and you know that I didn't and 'cause we're here to talk 'bout you." His lips drew back in a smile only slightly and his eyes were serious. He turned his face away from me and looked at the river.

"You know, you haven't told me anything I didn't already know, but somehow I feel better. I guess this means now you are my best friend," I said.

"Well, I'm not Keykey or your Daddy, but you got my number. You know that you can count on me."

"Wait a minute. I think Mom might consider you her best friend. Do you think she would mind sharing you?" I asked lightheartedly.

"Well, you would have to ask her." He again looked at me with a slight smile and raised his brow. "Teen knows I care about all four of y'all. Y'all as much my family as my parents, brothers and sisters."

I studied his profile as he gazed into the river. I knew he cared about all of us, but he seemed to care about Mom and me just a little bit more. He used to call me his chocolate princess. He didn't have pet names for my sisters, Laura and Angie.

I roused myself from my thoughts, "Well, one day, you're going to have to tell me how you and Daddy got to be such good friends," I said out loud.

He laughed and shook his head. "Not today."

I felt the breeze that carried with it a tiny bit of mist from the waters of Red River. I stood on the levee and stared at the beauty of the blue sky, pecan trees by the bank and far away fishermen with my best friend Adrian. He took my hand in his and when I started to say something, he said, "Sheee, let's just enjoy the view. We can't solve no mysteries today, so let's just enjoy the view."

CHAPTER 4

This is my favorite part of Christmas at home. I like decorating the tree with the girls," Ray said as he placed an ornament on the tree.

Ray, Delores and I were alone in the auditorium as we decorated for the Nighttime Christmas program. We'd been appointed to handle the program this year, and had put up a Christmas tree. Joy to the World played on the portable radio Ray had bought to soothe our minds as we worked.

"I like decorating the tree," I said. "My mom usually makes hot chocolate while we decorate. When I was small, we didn't have glass ornaments. We made ornaments with paper we'd colored, popsicle sticks we'd dyed, popcorn we'd strung together to make garland, whatever we could find." I paused. "Now, that I think about it, those were probably some very sad looking trees." I laughed. "At the time, we thought they were beautiful."

Ray'd changed into jeans and a turtle neck sweater so he could climb up the ladder to add ornaments and lights up high. The outfit accentuated his muscular frame. He had large brown eyes with long lashes most girls would die for, and a thin mustache over full lips. With eyes that probed my face, he said, "I bet they were beautiful. Because, after all, it's in the eye of the beholder."

"What's in the eye of the beholder?" Delores asked.

"Beauty," he replied. "Beauty is in the eye of the beholder. Somebody said that." His eyes surveyed me slowly as they traveled from my face and rested on my legs. As I felt the heat of his glance, my legs moved involuntarily, shifting from side to side. Heat rose to my face and I sneaked a look at Delores to see if she'd seen how he'd eyed me. I breathe a sigh of relief when I noticed she'd been busy with the ornaments.

"I mean, to a child looking at a tree they decorated for Christmas," he said, which brought me back to earth and made me wonder if I had misunderstood his stare.

He nodded his head and tightened his lips. "Man, I bet your tree was beautiful," he said and once again, he ogled me as if I were Christmas candy.

"Yes, you are right," I said as I brushed off his obvious meaning and focused on what we were supposed to be talking about, those long ago days.

He seemed to settle down and before we knew it, we were finished.

As she stood back from the tree, Delores said, "I think this is beautiful. I think we did a fantastic job."

I nodded. The lighted tree with its multi-colored lights, bows and angel on top, reflected in the shiny floors of the auditorium and it looked magnificent.

We unfurled a large roll of craft paper with a drawing of Mary, Joseph and Baby Jesus, and fastened it to the back curtains. The banner became a lovely backdrop for the program.

Again, we stepped back and beheld the tree and congratulated each other. Delores said, "That looks superb."

I said, "Yes, it does. Listening to Silent Night and looking at this beautiful setting, I honestly feel the Christmas spirit. We make a good team, you all."

Ray said, "Yes, we do. We make a very good team."

The next day the principal congratulated us on our setting and program. From then on, the three of us always sat together in meetings and in the break room. We became good friends.

∞

"I was in an antique shop in Alexandria yesterday. I saw the perfect manger for the Christmas program next year. Do you want to go out and see it tomorrow?" Ray asked when he called me at home during Easter Break.

My heart skipped a beat when I'd recognized his voice. I said, "I can't, Angie's home."

He answered quickly, "That's fine, bring her along."

"Well, she has been bored in the house and wanting some place to go," I said as I justified it in my mind. "Okay."

Nothing could happen in an antique shop in Alexandria. I thought. This is harmless, because Angie is coming with us.

Hence, the next day, I found myself at an antique store in Alexandria with Ray and Angie, my sister.

The antique store was filled with treasures. There were large fine furniture pieces and glass cabinets, which displayed lots of sparkling china and crystal. As we walked through the store, I imagined the splendid homes these mahogany pieces had adorned. He touched the richly colored beds and chests and I admired his fingers. They were long, graceful and manicured. I remembered how his hand had felt on mine when he'd opened the door for me on the first day of school.

"You have beautiful hands." The words escaped my lips before I realized it.

His head jerked in my direction, surprised, but he smiled, "Well, thank you." He took my hands in his and said, "Yours are beautiful also."

"How do you know?" I asked. "You're not looking at them."

"I don't have to. I know they are. Anyone with eyes like yours and with legs like yours has got to have beautiful hands," he whispered. My eyes were glued to his lips as if I were hypnotized.

Angie said as she joined us, "What are you all looking for?" I jumped and took a deep breath.

"It's over here," said Ray.

The manger was a small wooden structure shaped like the body of a tiny bassinet tinted brown. Ray was right. It was what we had searched for. He bargained a good deal for us and we bought it.

He said, "Angie, have you had a good time today?"

"It was all right. I guess it was better than staying home." I hadn't thought she'd had a good time as she followed us around, but I knew she had better manners than to tell him that.

He folded his arms and put his hand under his chin and said, "Well, before we leave Alexandria, what do you say about us going to buy you a record?"

"What? A record?" she grinned and jumped up and down.

"Yes, do you think you can find yourself a record you like?"

"Yes. Yes. Please." She said. I pressed my fingers to my smiling lips. I was so grateful he was doing something to make Angie feel like she was important.

We walked over to the record shop, which had aisles of counters with records displayed and stocked. Angie rushed to the part of the store where the forty-fives were and got busy examining them.

I said, "You are really something. How did you know she would love a forty-five? She has worn all of ours out."

"She has?" he asked. "Would you like one too?" His eyes held my gaze so strongly, it seemed like he wanted to penetrate my soul.

"No, I'm fine," I said as I looked away.

"You sure?"

"Yeah, I'm fine."

"Well, there was something for us and I thought there ought to be something for her. I know youngsters love music."

"Yeah, they do. Only thing is the manger is not really for us, it's for work," I said.

"Yes, it is for us. We got to spend time together. I got a chance to look into your gorgeous face today."

A short hollow laugh escaped my lips. "Okay, I have enjoyed today. I'm not going to lie about that. But, you know there can be nothing between us, Ray. We work together. I don't want to ruin our friendship with a relationship that's not going anywhere."

He said, "All I know is that I had a wonderful time today."

"This is a work trip and we, probably, shouldn't have come," I said. I struggled to find the right words. "I have to keep complications out of my life. God knows you have enough complications in yours," I said.

Angie walked up with her record choice, "Got the one I've wanted for a long time. It's not in the record shop in Marksville. Thank you so much, Mr. Dean. I'm so glad we came shopping here today."

∞

"Charlawt, wha' y'all do taday?" Mom asked, when I picked her up from Dr. Frank's house. I had not looked forward to this conversation.

"Angie and I went to Alexandria with Ray," I said. My mouth felt dry.

"Whatcha say?" my mother asked.

"Went to Alexandria, with Ray Dean," I answered as I squeezed the steering wheel.

"Dat what I thought ya said," her voice rose. "Haf ya gon plum crazy? Ya know dat man married. Dat rascal don't care if'n he puts ya in de family way, either."

"Oh Mom, it's not like that," I said. A sharp pain radiated through my head. "He just took us out for a pleasant day's drive and we took care of some business at the same time, that's all."

"Wha' y'all do in Alexandria?"

"We bought a manger for next year's play. Mom, I know you worry about me, but I'm grown now and I can take care of myself. I know how to tell a married man that I'm not interested in him and I did that. He know there can't be anything between us."

"Well, ya might not think dat way, but ya dunno what he think. Please, Charlawt, don't do dat no mo," she insisted. She turned to me and gave me an unwavering stare. "It's jes' not worth it. Only takes one mess up and everythin' fur you be diff'rent. Do ya git what Ah say. He a snake, I'm tellin' ya, dat man a snake in the grass."

"Mom, I am telling you, it's not going to happen again."

She mumbled under her breath, "Wan' be able ta walk around town wit' ya head up, messin' round wit' a married man. And ya know his wife strange. From Teresa's fam'ly."

"Your good friend, Miss Teresa?"

"Yeah, her niece."

"Uh huh," I said. "Why do you think she's strange?"

"Mos of 'em root doctors. You know, hoodoo. Lotsa folks go see 'em fur sickness 'n fur somethin' else."

"You mean, like hexing people?" I asked.

"Look, Ah knowed Teresa done he'p lotsa people who been sick 'n furs Ah knowed dat's all she do. No hexing, but others in 'er fam'ly do potions 'n mojo bags to hex people. Sos I'm a tellin' ya ta leave dat man alone. Can't work out ta ya good, no way, no how."

"I hear you Mama. I don't believe in that hoodoo stuff, but

nothing is going to happen with Ray, anyway."

"Don't b'lieve in it, huh? 'Member you was 'bout 'leven 'n ya had a rash in ya face 'n I took ya ta see n ole man? Member dat?"

"Yeah, I remember. After church, we went up to this old man who doesn't normally be at our church, and you told him about my rash and he chanted something, took a big swig of tobacco, chewed it and then spit it in my face. It took me by surprise. I couldn't move. And then he rubbed it in a circle."

"Um hum." She nodded. "Ya face cleared up, didn't it?"

"Yeah, it did, but how I know it wouldn't have cleared up on it's own?" I asked.

"Well, ya been had it, 'n didn't clear up. Dat's why Ah took ya ta 'im. Dat week it was clear. So ya kin b'lieve whatcha want. Ya healin' speaks fur itself. Bes' be safe then sorry. Ya don't need dat woman puttin' no hex on ya. I say, leave 'im be."

"I hear you Mom," I said.

CHAPTER 5

"Miss Ford, my husband and I are going to eat tonight at CBs Cafe and I was wondering if you'd like to join us?" Delores asked as we made copies of our final tests for the end of year in the school office.

"This is your date night, isn't it? Are you sure you want me to come?" I asked, tilted my head and paused.

She stopped fiddling with papers and said sincerely, "It'll be fine. Herb won't mind. I know you have been staying in since Keykey passed and I thought this might be a nice outing for you."

"I'd love to. I'll meet you there around six," I said, nodded my head and touched her on her arm.

After school, I drove two streets away from the school in the colored side of town. I arrived at a one-story brick building with four large plate glass windows, and a blinking neon sign that said CBs Café. I saw Delores already waiting for me inside. The walls were painted light brown with a string of red Christmas lights affixed to the top of the walls.

"Hi, there," she said and stood to greet me.

"Hey Girl," I responded. I sat beside her at a table covered with a red and white-checkered tablecloth. "It's been so long since I have been out. I really don't know how to act."

Delores was a short, medium sized woman, who smiled at everyone she met. She was several years older than me, and wore her hair in a bob.

"Really? Well, Herb and I come out once a week. My mom keeps the kids and sometimes we just ride around. Sometimes, we come out to eat, and sometimes, we go to a movie."

"Girl, that sounds good. I don't know," I began. I shook my head from side to side. "I really enjoy teaching, but occasionally, I feel lonely."

"You'll find somebody," she said.

"How am I going to do that? Who is there? Am I going to be Mrs. Carlton Thomas?" I said. Carlton Thomas was an elderly widower deacon in my church. "He tries to flirt with me anytime I am in his presence."

With her eyes big, she turned her head toward me suddenly, and then burst into laughter.

"Uh, Char, you can come sit by me," I said, as I mimicked Carlton's voice and patted the seat beside me. "I got some mustard greens I can bring by your house after church. You gonna be home?"

Delores laughed until tears started to come out of her eyes. She said, "Please stop, Girl, you are killing me."

I joined her in laughter and when we stopped, I said, "You and Herb's been married now about six years. Right?"

"Yeah, right out of college," she answered.

"You were a senior, when I was a freshman in college. Do you remember Robert Jackson?" I asked. "He was a senior also."

"Yeah, I remember him. About your height, good looking guy. Snazzy dresser. He was married, wasn't he? Well, he got married or something like that."

"All of the above," I said. "He wasn't married when we met.

We fell in love. Well, I did anyway. Then, his girl back home, got pregnant and he had to marry her. To make a long story short, he said he didn't love her, and I, like a fool, continued to go with him for the rest of my college years."

"But he graduated when I did," Delores added.

"Yeah, he did. But, he continued to come to Grambling on weekends for football games, dances, and basketball games. Instead of cultivating a relationship with an eligible guy, I took up my precious time with this sleaze ball. It didn't bother me, because I really wasn't concerned about getting married. Mom always stressed to me how important it was to be able to take care of myself and not depend on anyone else to take care of me. All I cared about was getting a degree."

"What happened? Why are you not together now?"

"Once I was through college, he was still married. No more homecomings, or special activities to come to. I came back to Marksville. Couldn't bring a married man to Mom's house, so it ended. I have been okay, but since Keykey passed, I wish I would have done things differently."

"We've known each other a long time, Charlotte. We grew up in the same small neighborhood. We share some of the same struggles, like working our way through college. You are a very strong lady. Someone will come along. Wait a minute." She stopped and cocked her head to one side, "What about Adrian Fonteneau?"

"Adrian?" I asked surprised.

"Yeah, whenever he's in town, he's always at your mom's house. I remember him coming to see you at Grambling. And he was so good looking, with his slim build, curly hair, hazel eyes and smooth complexion. All the girls in the dorm would go wild. I used to think something was going on between him and your mom, but you said no. So, isn't he available?"

"Yeah, he's available, but Adrian's my buddy, my pal.

Nothing's going on with Mom because she always said he was too young for her. He's ten years younger than she is, you know. Plus, he was my daddy's best friend and I don't know what we would do without him. Besides that, he is nineteen years older than me."

"Well, a good friendship is an extremely good start. He's in real good shape even if he is nineteen years older than you are. You know what I mean?" She looked at me, winked and ran her tongue slowly over her lips, and then uttered a throaty growl. We both erupted in laughter again.

"Delores, you know you're wrong," I said jokingly. "Well, he doesn't see me like that either."

Her husband, Herb Batiste, joined us at our table.

I looked out the window and couldn't believe my eyes. Ray drove up and got out of his car. My heart quickened. I prayed he would not come into the café, but he did. Once in the restaurant, he walked casually over to our table.

"Hey Man, what's going on?" Herb said. He stood up and they shook hands. "Me, my ole lady and Charlotte came out to eat. Would you like to join us?"

I held my breath. I hoped Ray would decline the invitation.

"I'd love to, if it's okay with everyone." he said without hesitation. I got a sinking feeling in my stomach.

Ray nodded at Delores and me. "Charlotte, Delores," he said.

I nodded back and averted my eyes.

"My wife doesn't like to go out. So, I'm on my own a lot of the time," he said and looked directly at Herb.

Herb looked at him and raised an eyebrow, "Trouble on the home front, Man."

"No no," said Ray. "I let her do what makes her happy, Man. I don't bother her. I entertain myself and long as I don't bother her, we get along fine."

I had a giddy feeling. Could this mean I was glad to see Ray? I sure hope not. These thoughts ran through my mind. I wanted to leave and I wanted to stay all at the same time. I couldn't leave, because it would look suspicious to Herb and Delores.

"How's the fried fish?" Ray asked me after our food was served.

"Delicious, simply delicious," I answered.

He said, in almost a whisper, "Say that again."

I drew my brows together and said, "Delicious, simply delicious."

"I just love the way you say that. The word delicious seems to just roll off of your tongue," he said in a low husky voice.

I buried my eyes into my plate and then, looked up and glared at him. What is he doing? I thought. Herb and Delores were sitting at the table and I didn't want them to get the wrong idea.

"Now, Ray, are you okay? Are you hallucinating or something?" I asked.

He laughed, "No, I'm not hallucinating. I'm really not. I could have sworn you said something else, and it turned out to be delicious. I just have never heard it said quite that way before." Then in the same husky voice, "Say it again."

"Stop it, Ray," I snapped, and glanced at Herb and Delores, who both sat with their eyes on us with small smiles on their faces. They were anxious to see what would happen next.

"Just messing with you," he said. "Wanted to ruffle your feathers, that's all. You're always so prim and proper."

"Ooh, you're incorrigible," I said. "Worse than your students."

Herb and Delores laughed out loud. "Man, don't do that. Charlotte was 'bout to jump outta that plate glass window to get 'way from you," Herb said as he continued to laugh.

Delores patted me on my hand to show her support.

"I'm all right," I said. "Will you all please excuse me for a minute?" I left the table to go to the bathroom.

I looked up as I washed my hands and in the bathroom

mirror, I saw a tall slim lady, with short curly black hair, and wearing a figure fitting dress. She stood behind me and our eyes met in the mirror. I knew her to be Renée Black from St. Mary's Church. "Hi Charlotte. How are you?"

"Fine Renée. How are you?" I turned to face her.

"I'm fine. Look, I don't want to interfere, but I saw you sitting with Ray Dean. I would like to warn you to not be fooled by his so called caring ways. He is a user and a liar and a womanizer," she said as she accentuated womanizer. "Please be careful."

I wondered why she was telling me these things. Then I realized she thought Ray and I were together because we sat as one of two couples at the table.

"No need to warn me against Ray. He is a fellow co-worker and friend. That is the only reason he is at the table. There is nothing of a romantic nature between us."

"I have seen you two together before and you always look so into each other. I'm just saying, he is married and he is not going to leave his wife. No matter what he tells you." She paused a minute. "I have a daughter for him and he was single when I got pregnant," she said. "When his now wife found out about it, she was upset and decided to leave town and to persuade her to stay, he married her. So, he sacrificed being with my child and me. He has had affairs with other people since, and they all end the same way. He stays with his wife, Seraphine, and if he tells you different, he's lying. You seem like a nice lady. I just thought you should know."

She turned and walked out of the bathroom and left me there with my mouth open.

Every word she'd said resonated with me and I felt pangs of disappointment. Why am I hurt by what she said? I have no right to feel jealous of his relationship with another woman. Mixed in with jealousy was empathy, because I also understood how she felt.

When the meal was over, Ray walked me to my car. I told him what had happened in the bathroom. He listened and never interrupted me.

"Renée does have a child for me," he replied.

I said, "I don't need any explanations. I just wanted you to know what had been said about you. That's all."

"I want to tell you about it," he said. We reached our cars. "You mean a lot to me and I want you to understand what happened. I know she is hurt and I am sorry for that. She and I were not in a relationship. I know that is no excuse, but I thought she was on birth control. Again, no excuse. I feel sorry about what happened between us and I do provide child support for our child."

"Like I said, this is really none of my business."

He lightly touched my hand and said softly, "I really want you to understand what happened. Don't let what other people say about me turn you against me. Trust your judgment and not someone else's."

His eyes willed me to believe him and to see him as a man and not just a co-worker or friend. My determination began to soften. He was close enough for me to smell his after-shave. His touch both frightened and excited me.

"Ok, I hear what you're saying. I have to get home. My mother worries when I'm late."

I got in my car and did not look back at him. I think he thought I was angry because of what Renée had said. I was not. I just needed to keep my distance.

∞

On Saturday afternoon, I answered the phone, in my mother's living room, and discovered Ray on the line.

"Hi Charlotte. I want to talk to you about something. It won't take much of your time, I promise."

"So talk," I answered as I looked out my window.

"Not on the phone. Please meet me in the park."

"No way. That's asking for trouble."

"It'll only take an hour of your time. At the most. Please."

"I guess I can spare an hour. Only an hour. This is against my better judgment. But okay, I'll meet you in an hour."

As I drove up, he stood by a tree in blue jeans, knit shirt and tennis shoes near a sidewalk. People walked around the park at the far end, but he was the only person in the area where he stood. As I approached him, he smiled and I got a little flutter in the pit of my stomach and warned myself to be careful.

"Hi Charlotte. Thank you for coming," he said. He handed me a present. It was a book of love poems. "I noticed when we were on bus duty together you liked to read poems, so I picked this up for you. Hope you like them."

"Oh, thank you very much Ray. I love to read books period, but a small book like this I can bring with me when I know I have to wait somewhere. Thank you so much. You are very observant and thoughtful."

"I felt uneasy about what Reneé told you. She came into my life when I was young and impulsive. I had to choose between her and my wife and I felt closer to my wife at the time. Because like I said, there wasn't a relationship. So, I married my wife, Seraphine. Now, my wife and I have nothing in common, except the children. And I know you said it doesn't matter, but I care what you think."

We walked down a path that led to an area where trees more densely grew. Spring was here and the earth was alive with vegetation and my body also began to come awake after a long sleep. The walkway was mostly shrubbery, but every now and then there were patches of flowers. I felt the beauty of the surroundings as it entered my soul.

"Ray, I'm sorry your marriage is not what you would like it to be."

"Charlotte, the only reason I am still married is because of my children. We don't socialize together, or talk, or sleep together for that matter."

"Ray, I am so sorry."

"I love my kids, Charlotte. I'm not leaving my kids."

"I know you love your kids. You speak of them anytime we are together.

"I am not close to my daughter by Reneé, because she hates me so much and makes it quite difficult for me to see her."

As we reached a fork in the path, he caught my hand and steered me to go to the left. He did not let it go afterward.

We entered a wooded area, still engrossed in conversation and stopped. "You have been a light in my life. I can't wait to see you in the morning and you are the last thing I think about at night." He leaned in and kissed me.

I just stood there. I seemed mesmerized. I wanted to pull away, but didn't. His lips were so soft, and it had been so long since I'd been kissed. He kissed me again, this time deeply. My senses cried out to me: oh my God, what in the world is happening?

His arms encircled me as we continued to kiss.

Then, wisdom returned and I pulled away. "I'm sorry, but this cannot happen again," I said.

He stared at me and said calmly, "Ok. If that's what you want."

"That's what I want."

We walked back to my car in silence. He opened my door and said in a light tone, "See you Monday."

"Ok, thanks again for the book." I started my car and did not look at him. Driving away, my heart was beating so loud I couldn't hear my radio. I still felt the pressure and the warmth of his lips. Why had I let him kiss me? I admonished myself in my thoughts.

Then I resolved that this could not happen again.

Then the school year was over and I felt a sense of relief. I would not have to see him again until September.

CHAPTER 6

As I drove on the Rainbow Bridge in Bridge City, Texas, my knuckles were white on the steering wheel, because I squeezed it so hard. On the contrary, Angie looked out of the window and smiled from ear to ear. All I could see was the road, the blue sky and the railings that bordered the bridge.

"Wow, Char, this is so cool," she beamed in wonderment. "How far up in the air did you say we are?"

"According to the encyclopedia, we went fifty four miles up in the air. Thank goodness, we're almost off the bridge now." It was like riding on a roller coaster. But I didn't let it show. I didn't want to scare Angie. "We should be at Laura's house in Port Arthur, Texas, very soon."

"This is just the best summer vacation ever. Going to visit Laura and the kids. Laura is the best sister ever. Well, next to you that is," she said.

I laughed, "Yes, she is a sweet sister and we don't get to see each other or talk often enough. Long distance calls are so expensive." And I won't run into Ray Dean in Texas, I thought.

We drove up in front of a small white house with shrubs that circled the porch. Laura was sitting on the front porch, waiting for us. She ran off the porch to greet us.

Angie and I hugged her laughing. My niece, Catherine and nephews, Lonny and Anthony ran around from the back yard. They called out, "You're here. You're here."

"Char, I swear, every time I see you, looks like you're taller. Am I right about that?"

"No, Laura, just because you're about five feet three inches doesn't mean I'm getting taller. But, I declare Angie looks like a younger you. Y'all about the same height, same light complexion, same wavy hair, same build and everything."

Laura smiled and looked at Angie, "Come here, Baby Sister, and give me another hug. I'm a good person for you to look like. I'm your big sister."

"So, why do I look so different? I'm your sister, too." I hadn't meant to say that out loud and wished I could take it back.

Laura eyes left Angie's face and alighted on mine. "I don't know, Char. That's a question for God. Besides, you have Mom's eyes and hair." Then, in almost a whisper, she asked, "You still wonder about that?"

"No, not really," I said as I avoided her eyes.

We walked into the house through the living room and went into the kitchen. The air was filled with tantalizing smells of food. Laura had a large pot of stew on the stove. It was a large eat-in kitchen and we all sat around the table.

"Girl, the house looks wonderful," I said as I admired the soft light yellow wallpaper that covered most of the house. "You are an amazing housekeeper," I continued as I also admired the shiny vinyl gray floors. "Despite the fact you work as a LPN."

"Thank you very much," she said

∞

After we dropped the kids off at a nearby Y, Laura and I sat down to talk.

"You can still burn. That stew was off the charts good," I said.

"Thank you. You know that's Mom's recipe."

"Well, Mom's stew is good. It may be because I was hungry, but I believe yours was better. Don't tell her I said that." We both laughed. "How are you doing? You seem a little down."

"It shows, huh. I try to keep it hidden so the kids won't worry. Rick has been very unpredictable lately. He's been drinking more lately. You know when he is not drinking, he is the sweetest thing. But when he is drinking, he is frightening."

"Frightening?"

"Yes, he is. He's getting worse. We've been married for fifteen years, but sometimes I think I might have to leave him. But when I think about leaving, I don't know where to go."

"Well, you can come home. You can always come home. I know you have gotten used to living in a city with city conveniences, but you wouldn't have to stay forever. Come home, get on your feet, put some distance between the two of you. Then, maybe, things will even out a little bit and you could move back," I said.

"Yeah, well, I know I can come home, which means I'll have to leave my job. No job means how am I going to feed three kids. I can't expect Mom to take care of me and three children. Plus whenever I talk about leaving, he threatens to hurt me and Mom."

"Mom?" I asked disbelievingly.

"Yeah, he threatens Mom all the time. For some reason, he thinks if I leave him, it's because Mom told me to and he's said he will kill her," she added.

I looked at her in disbelief. I realized how serious this was and I could not believe we were in this kind of situation. "You are serious, aren't you? Has he hit you?" I asked.

She took a deep breath. "Yes, he has."

"Oh my God!" I said. "I had no idea you were going through this. Whenever we talk with you, everything sounds great. Has he ever hit the kids?"

"No, not yet. But Lonny gets so angry when he hits me and I am afraid Rick will hurt him for standing up for me."

Laura got up and sliced a piece of cake for each of us.

"Well, what are you going to do? You surprise me Laura. You act like him hitting you is ok. You'll only leave if he hits the kids?" I asked, desperation sneaking into my voice.

"I don't know. Most of the time, he is ok. Especially after he does something bad. He tries to compensate for what he's done and he is overly nice and pleasing until something happens, at work, or for some other reason. The problem is I don't know what will set him off. He will get upset about something and then get a bottle and then the upheaval begins. I don't think it is okay for him to hit me. I just don't know what to do about it."

"Have you talked to his parents about it? The times I met them they seemed like honest hard working people. In fact, his father seemed like a gentle man."

"I tried one time. His parents were very understanding and concerned for the kids and me. They were shocked by his behavior. When they talked to him about it, he downplayed everything. Then he assured them he would be more considerate of the kids and me. They believed him. Believe me, I felt the force of his wrath after that and I never mentioned anything to them again. I think he is disappointed in himself. I think he saw himself achieving more in life than he has and on some level he also blames me for that. Because we got married so young, you know."

"Have you called the police?"

"Once, I tried and he stood in front of me and told me if I called the police, I would be dead by the time they got here. And from the look in his eyes, Char, I believed him."

I said, "Girl, you need a plan on how to get out of here and away from him. You are not a psychiatrist. You cannot help him."

"I know what you're saying. His face just looks like the devil himself whenever he is in that zone."

We heard a key in the door and Rick walked in and placed his lunch box on a kitchen cabinet. His clothes, face and hands were dirty from work and he walked with his head down. His eyes widened when he saw me and he smiled. "Hi Char, it's good to see you. Did you have a good drive?" His face and arms were a deep brown from working in the sun.

Laura got up and walked over to him and stood on tiptoes and kissed him on the cheek.

I said, "Yes, I did. The weather was beautiful, but the bridge at Orange, Texas blew my mind."

He laughed, "I know it did. You probably peed your pants." Then to Laura, "Baby, think I'm ready for that stew. Had a rough day today." Then he directed his words to me, "Being a longshoreman is tough, Char."

"All right, Sweetie," she said. "It's just like you like it."

"Thanks, Baby." He leaned over and said something in her ear. She smiled and nodded.

I sat there and watched them. How she called him Sweetie and how he whispered kind endearments to her. There is no way I would guess they had big time marital problems. Rick was about six feet and very muscular. I imagined how much it must hurt whenever he decided to hit her. My heart ached for her.

In spite of what I had just learned, I sat with Rick as he ate his supper. "Rick, I remember the first time I saw you. I was a little girl, seven or eight years old. You would come by our house to see Laura. You were always friendly and I thought you were the best looking thing I'd ever seen. Remember that?"

"Char, thank you for the compliment. I don't think I knew that you thought I was good-looking," he smiled seeming to be genuinely pleased, "but I do remember coming by your house. Your mom wouldn't let me and Laura go nowhere by ourself. We had to bring you with us," he said.

"Yes, you did. I enjoyed those dates. Made me feel like a big girl. That's the way it was back then, Rick. A decent young lady did not go out on a date not chaperoned. Mom was protecting Laura from being tempted, but mainly, from gossip from the small town busy bodies. There were a lot of those. Just waiting to see how they could spoil a young girl's reputation."

"Yeah, I guess so. But from the first time I laid eyes on 'er, I knew I was gonna marry 'er and I did."

"Yes, you did. And look where you are now. Beautiful home and three beautiful children." Things were quiet between us for a second while he continued to eat.

"I know you're right, Char. But I thought I would've been a foreman by now, stead of still reportin' to the union hall to find out where or if I'm gonna work, like everybody else. Know what I mean? The cats on the dock not easy to work with. Can't seem to break out of that box."

"Sweetie," said Laura. "You thinking about doing something different?"

"No, didn't say that. Just sometimes, things get rough on the docks. That's all I'm saying. It's a dog eats dog out there. Well, I'm pooped. So Char, I'll talk with you tomorrow."

"Okay, Rick." Laura and I exchanged looks. There would be no more talk about his abuse tonight, not while he was in earshot.

∞

"Oh Sweetie, you're home. I didn't know," said Laura to Rick when he came home from work. We'd sat on her back porch after we'd finished barbecuing on Friday. It was a serene and peaceful atmosphere. Rose bushes occupied one fence line and a pecan tree grew along the other fence line.

Rick put his hand up and placed his hand in front of Laura's chest to stop her from kissing him. "Why don't you know? Huh, tell me, why don't you know?" His eyes darted toward the food, then at me and back to Laura.

"Well, we are in the backyard and I didn't hear the front door," she said, with her hands outstretched as if she wanted him to come into her arms.

"Know you didn't expect me this early. What were you and Char planning to do?" he continued in a menacing voice.

"We were doing what we planned to do. We played with the kids, ate and we're going to bed early," she said.

"Where did y'all go today? Did y'all go see y'all men?"

"Men?" said Laura. "What are you talking about?"

"Talking 'bout the odometer. My odometer on my car say y'all went to see y'all men today."

"We stayed home today. Didn't bring the kids anywhere, Sweetie."

"Don't Sweetie, me. Why don't you do something with your hair and lose some weight. Tired of looking at your fat ass."

I stood up involuntarily, because I wanted to protect her from his hurtful, stinging denigrations. His words stung me as though I'd been hit in my chest. His eyes darted quickly to me and for a moment, I thought he was going to turn his venom toward me. But he looked back at Laura.

Her face and her shoulders fell. She dabbed at her eyes, but then threw her head, tossing her long hair, raised her shoulders up, pushed her chest forward and said, "My hair is like you always told me you liked it, loose down my back," in a strong voice.

"Well, that is what you're telling me now. But, whatcha planning to do? I know Feen told Char to tell you to leave me. She'd better stay out of my business." He seemed to get more agitated as each minute passed.

Now, I understood what Laura meant about Ricky's fixation with Mom. Out of the blue, he blamed her for his situation.

Mom is not even here. She is in another state. My heart continued to beat fast and I began to take large breaths. I told myself to stay calm, because getting angry was not going to help. In fact, it would make things worse.

Everyone was silent. Laura was trying to let things cool down. Our eyes met and she shook her head at me when Rick wasn't looking which signaled me to stay quiet. Tension was palpable in the air and I was as upset as Laura. After all, he'd insulted my sister and my mom.

"Laura, where is my plate?" he asked.

She walked over to the barbecue pit and began to fix him a plate.

He said, "Didn't tell you I wanted any. Just asked you where it was. And since I see you gotta fix it. Means it wasn't fixed already and put in the oven to keep warm for me to get it, if I came home late. Y'all were just going to eat it all."

"Ricky, don't be ridiculous," she said.

"What? What? Who you calling ridiculous? Are you telling me I'm ridiculous, you whore?" His voice had risen steadily until it was a shrill scream. His veins were huge in his neck and he moved toward her with his fist in the air.

Laura eyes and mouth opened and I made a step forward.

Their son, Lonny, who was fourteen, ran into the back yard, giving Laura a chance to move out of his range. "What's wrong, Daddy?" he asked. "What's wrong, Daddy? Did you have a bad day on the docks?" Lonny was big for his age and muscular for a boy his size. He played on his high school football team.

Rick's head turned quickly toward him, squished his eyebrows together and rubbed his chin. After several long seconds that felt like minutes, he nodded his head, turned and walked back into the house and to his bedroom.

Lonny went to his mother, hugged her and said, "It's all right. Nothing happened."

I felt like I'd held my breath forever and now I exhaled. I'd witnessed what Laura was putting up with. Indeed, he was frightening. He became a whole different person. I whispered to her, "You have to leave him. I don't know what his problem is, but you have your kids to protect."

Lonny said, "I'll go back in now. We were playing cards and it's probably my play by now. Are you ok, Mom?"

"Yes, Baby. Go on back to your game."

She turned to me and said, "Do you see what I'm talking about? He's getting worse. Usually, he doesn't do that in front of people. He would have waited until you had gone home. And this is outside." She stood with her hands out from her side, looking all around as if she could see all her neighbors peering from their backyards.

"He was screaming and calling me names where our neighbors could hear." She shook her head and started to cry. "He is getting worse. I really don't know what to do, anymore. I am really getting scared."

I put my arms around her and said, "We are supposed to leave tomorrow. Do you want to come with us? You could get a job at the hospital in Pineville."

"No, I'm not ready to leave my job."

"Do you want us to stay?" I was at a loss. I wanted to stay, but I was not sure that would help.

"Oh no, this is my problem to solve. But thank you."

"But Laura, are you sure?" I insisted. "I don't know if I can leave you like this." I turned her towards me and took her shoulders into my hands and our eyes locked. I wanted to shake her, but didn't.

She shook her head, "There is nothing you can do. I know I have to get my kids to safety. I will let you know if I need you to do something. Okay?" she answered.

"What do you plan to do?" I asked.

"I'm not sure right now. I don't know how I will do it, but I know now that I have to leave. I will let you know if I need your help. Do you understand?"

I had no choice but to accept what she was saying. She was, after all, a grown person and I have to trust she knows the best way to handle this situation.

Rick joined us in the living room as we watched TV at nine o'clock. When he entered, the kids quickly went to their rooms. He walked directly to Laura and laid his head in her lap. Laura stiffened. "Sugar, I'm so sorry. I didn't mean nothing I said."

Laura didn't answer. She gazed straight ahead. "Please Sugar, forgive me. You are so beautiful and sweet."

Laura said, "You mean my fat ass is beautiful and sweet."

A flush of adrenalin raced through my body and I jumped. That was the first hint of anger I'd seen from Laura since we got here. "Aw, Sugar, you know I didn't mean that. You are the right size for me. You know I like a little meat on my women. I need you, please forgive me."

"That's what you say every time, Rick. And then something happens on the docks and I pay for it," she continued.

Rick shifted his attention to me. "Char, I'm sorry that happened in front of you. Am I still your favorite brother-in-law?"

Still a little angry, I decided it was best not to show it. "Yes, you are definitely still my favorite brother-in-law." Daring to venture further, I said, "Do you think counseling with…"

Laura cut me off by drawing our attention to a show on television, "Look y'all, the old lady won five thousand dollars."

Everyone's attention moved to the TV show and with Rick looking at the television show, our eyes met and she shook her head letting me know not to mention counseling.

Rick said, "We'll talk later. Go on and watch your show. I'm going to get me something to eat." He went into the stove oven, got his plate and ate it before he joined us in the living room again. I wasn't sure if Rick was truly sorry and I hated to leave Laura.

CHAPTER 7

*D*o ya thin' she be's all right, Bay?" My mother said worried as I filled her in on what had happened when we visited Laura. We were sitting on our front porch.

"I don't know, Mom," I said.

"Ah had no idea Rick was lack dat. I'm going to call 'er and tell 'er to come home. No need'n 'er puttin' up with no man beatin' on 'er. Mos of'n don't change," she said.

"Funny thing, Mom, I always thought she was so lucky to be married to a man like Rick. It boggles my mind to find out her marriage is completely different than I thought. The old saying about 'No one knows what goes on behind closed doors.' is definitely true about this. And he has such a kind hearted manner," I said. I wondered how someone who looks like he does could bring such misery.

"Well, my mama used to say, 'Ever'thin' dat shines ain' gold.' Ah know my gran' chil'ren can't live lack dat."

I remembered Rick's threat about my mother and hurriedly said, "Mom, we have to stay out of it. Laura told me that she has a plan and she will let me know what I can do to help her."

"Ah can't stan' de thought of my chile bein' hurt and Ah can't do nothin' ta he'p her. Gonna call 'er mo. Long distance is so s'pensive, but haf ta keep in touch somehow."

"We have to trust her Mom. You raised her right and she is not going to let him hurt those kids. Although, she seems to be allowing him to hurt her. If she doesn't do something by Christmas, maybe we can go to visit. Okay?"

"Char, if you say so. Ah jes' don't feel good 'bout it. Lawd, haf mercy on my chile in danger, way yonder in Port Arthur, Texas. Where Ah can't git ta her easy. I'm puttin' 'er in yo hands, Lawd," she said with her head down and her eyes closed.

As she prayed, I walked back inside of the house and said a prayer myself.

∞

Soon, it was the Fourth of July. I rode down the narrow streets of Marksville's town square and found a good location to park my car, so I could sit on the hood and watch the annual parade.

Surprise flooded my senses when I spotted Ray standing across the street. He had his children with him. I adjusted my straw hat so I could look in his direction without him knowing it. But I tried not to look over where he stood. As cars and floats filled with young white girls in gowns waved as they passed and high school bands played music and marched to the beat, I tried to concentrate on the parade. Most of the time, Ray watched the parade, but every now and then, I caught him staring at me. He looked away whenever our eyes met.

At the end of the parade, a car with two large glitter decorated poster boards affixed to each side, passed by. The sign said "St. Mary's Church". The car was draped with crepe paper of different colors. Behind the car were colored ladies walking in formation of five ladies across, dressed in white suits, gloves and shoes. I know they were hot in those outfits, but they marched on with their chins forward. They seemed to be marching to the beat of music that they heard in their own heads. Lord, have mercy, I thought. Why do they always put us at the end of the parade. They walked along, unsmiling. Folks applauded them, including me, as they passed by. Only one white man called them names. They marched on, looking straight ahead, as though they didn't hear him and everyone else ignored him. Since this was the last group, the crowd began to disperse.

Ray and his children crossed the street and approached me.

"Hi there, Mr. Dean. Hi," I said as I nodded to his children.

I looked at his oldest daughter and asked, "Did you enjoy the parade?" She's such a pretty little girl, I thought.

"Yes ma'am."

The rest of his children talked and laughed with each other, and paid no attention to us.

"Miss Ford, some friends of mine and a few teachers are going over to the park around seven tonight to just hang out and wait for the fireworks. If you're free, why don't you swing by?"

"Some teachers? What teachers? Is Miss Batiste going to be there?"

"I'm not sure about Miss Batiste. I know Miss Davis is going to be there."

"Well, I'll think about it. Okay?"

"All right. Should be fun. Hope to see you there," he said.

When seven o'clock rolled around, I paced back and forth in my room. I decided Ray would be on his best behavior if other people surrounded us. He'd said other people were going to be there, so I decided to go.

I arrived after seven and saw Ray's car parked in the same place it was the last time we were here. He stepped out of his car as I drove up. I could see no one else was here.

"Hi there, Beautiful," he said as he took my hand into his and kissed it.

I started to feel uneasy. "Where is everyone? Am I too late?"

"No, you're not late. I said that for two reasons. One. If you thought someone else was coming, you'd feel it was okay to come. Two. I wanted my daughter to think other people were coming. Just in case she mentions it to her mother," he said.

My mind went blank and I was speechless. My legs did not feel like they were a part of me and I could not move. I did not know if I should run, slap his face, or stay. He had manipulated me and had even misled his children.

He saw I was upset. His lips poked out and his eyes pleaded with me, "Walk with me a minute and then if you want to go, you know you can go. I would never stop you from leaving if you want to leave."

I knew that was true. He would let me leave if I wanted to, so I decided to walk with him. At first, no one said anything.

"I can't do this with you," I said and turned to leave.

"Wait. I understand. Stay just a little longer."

"I've been here before," I said. Yet, still I turned back around and continued to walk with him.

"What do you mean by that?"

"Dead end relationship when I was in college. A long term relationship that ended and left me with nothing to show for it."

"You are so special and I will never hurt you. Everything about you, the sassy walk you have, those big beautiful legs."

"Ray, I know you are a smart man, and a kind man. I know you love your children and you are a very attractive man and you know it. However, you are m a r r i e d." I said as I spelled out married.

We reached the wooded area where we had been before and there were a blanket and a basket with wine, chocolates, cheese and crackers, and one red rose.

He said, "I didn't know if you would stay, but if you did, I thought it would be nice to have wine and celebrate the Fourth together."

My mind flip-flopped and sent out warning signals, but I disregarded them and said, "I can stay for a little while, but you know I have to get home soon. Since I'm driving, I can only have one glass."

"Charlotte, I am not that other guy. I will not keep you dangling on a string for years. I won't hurt you like that."

We sat on the blanket and he opened the wine and poured each of us a glass of wine. He cut two pieces of cheese and gave me a piece with a cracker on a napkin.

"I understand what you're saying, but it is more to it than that and you know it."

"Trust me. Better yet, trust yourself. You know what you're feeling right now. Give in to it," he whispered.

"I don't know if I can do that." I answered as I ate the cheese and sipped the wine.

"Yes, you can." He unwrapped a piece of chocolate and placed it to my lips. I opened my lips and let him place it in my mouth. The bittersweet taste of the chocolate was tantalizing as it melted.

Because of the trees, it was quiet and cool in this location. The intense expression on his face telegraphed me that he was going to kiss me. It was like slow motion and I wanted to turn away, but I didn't. He leaned forward and kissed me and I kissed him back. He continued to kiss me and it felt so good just to let go and not be on guard. He unbuttoned my blouse and fondled my breast and then we lay down on the blanket as he continued to kiss me. He kissed me over and over until I felt as though I was floating on air.

He whispered in my ear, "Can I make love to you?"

"Yes. Please hold me close, before I float away." I'd said yes, because I wanted this glorious feeling to last.

"Don't worry. I got you."

We made love under the trees in the park. Afterwards, we lay on the blanket on our backs and watched the fireworks as they exploded in the sky, and turn into little streaks of different colored lights. Then each light would sail on going it's own separate way until it disappeared. He held my hand as though he was holding on for dear life, and he would never let it go.

I was reared in the church and knew it was a sin to make love out of wedlock. To make love to a married man was scandalous. I had vowed not to repeat that journey. Yet, here I was again. I did not know what I was going to do about it. I decided not to worry about it right now. I enjoyed the moment and remembered the feel of his lips and body.

He asked me, "Are you glad we made love?"

"Yes, I wanted to. It was wonderful. I'm not sure if I want it to happen again, but today was wonderful. The chocolates were divine. It seems that the way to my heart is through chocolates," I quipped.

When we walked back to our cars, he continued to hold my hand. He pulled me to him, placed a short kiss on my lips and whispered, "You are so lovely. You absolutely take my breath away." He placed the basket with what remained of our private picnic on the back seat of my car.

"Take care on the way home."

Our eyes locked, but I did not answer. The pull of him was still real and I did not want to dampen the mood. However, it was time for it to end. I turned and got into my car and drove away. I watched him in my rearview mirror. I wanted to turn the car around and return to his blissful arms, but I continued forward

When I got home, I gave the remaining chocolates to Angie. I fixed myself a nightcap with the rest of the wine and thought about my evening. My body was still alive, because we'd made love. I hugged myself and reveled in the feeling. One part of me could hardly wait for the next time, and the other part of me felt this could not happen again.

CHAPTER 8

Almighty God, what have I done? Please forgive me. I have developed strong feelings for a married man. I may even be in love with him. I need to lose those feelings. Please let there be no long lasting consequence. These were the prayers that occupied my mind in the days that followed the exhilarating experience in the park. As time passed and the glow wore off, the lightness of spirit that had given me joy slowly turned heavy as if a storm was drawing near.

Ray did not call or try to seek me out the rest of the summer.

Then summer was over and it was time to get back to the hustle and bustle of school. During the school's customary workshop for teachers, Ray, Delores and I sat together. The atmosphere was tense with a lot of awkward silences. Poor Delores seemed uncomfortable, unaware of the reason for the change in atmosphere.

When Ray and I met in the hall and out of earshot of everyone, he said, "I'm not sure how we should act. Every time I see you, I think about how lovely and sweet you are." His eyes were focused on my lips.

"Ray, please stop. Don't say anymore." I begged. I fought the warm glow that surged in my body, as his eyes reminded me of our passion. That feeling was followed by a punch in my stomach, because I also remembered he had not called me afterward.

He averted his eyes and nodded, "All right, you are probably right."

He actually appeared to be relieved that I released him from any obligation to continue our secret relationship.

After that meeting, whenever we passed each other in the hallways or in workshops, I avoided meeting his eyes. I felt so conflicted. However, neither Ray nor I made an effort to replay the events of July Fourth. I was saddened in a way, but I was also glad. It was for the best that we let this relationship die a natural death.

On the tenth of September, as my mother cooked bacon in the kitchen, the world spun in front of my eyes. My stomach turned over and a rush of liquid from my stomach attempted to enter my mouth. I ran into the bathroom and vomited. I sat on the toilet lid, with my eyes closed, trying to regain my equilibrium. When I attempted to rise again, my world spun again and I saw little white stars before my eyes. I sat with my head on my lap. Panic set in and I asked myself, what in the world is going on? Could I be pregnant? I am late on my period and have been really tired lately.

I heard my mother call me to come to breakfast and I couldn't answer her. I burst into tears. My thoughts raced. It had happened one time. Lord, just one time. Why do I have to pay so heavily for one mistake?

The last teacher who had gotten pregnant out of wedlock at this school was fired on the spot.

No, this can't be. Not now, not like this. I won't be able to walk around town without hearing the whispers behind my back. I'd attended college through scholarships, loans and work-study programs and had earned the respect of my town. Now to be fired in disgrace. But most of all, I did not want to disappoint my mother?

If only I were married? Ray is already married. Even if by some miracle he would agree to get a divorce, he couldn't get it done in time. The baby would be due around March or April and I will be showing way before that. Whom can I marry? Who would marry someone who is already pregnant with someone else's baby? I finally got the strength to answer Mom. "Not hungry."

"Ya all right, ya sho ya don' wanna eat."

"I'm all right, Mom. I'm sure I don't want to eat."

I hoped some fresh air would help, so I sat on the porch, which in my hometown is also called gallery, with my eyes closed. Then I read my book of poems, but the words passed by my eyes and they held no depth or meaning. After a poem or two, I realized I did not remember what I'd just read. I heard a car stop and looked up to see Adrian Fonteneau in his Chevrolet.

"Hi Adrian. Drove in from Houston today?" I asked, not meeting his eyes, hoping he didn't see the redness in mine.

"What's going on, Char? Yeah, this morning. Only here for a few days. Whatcha reading?"

"A book of poems somebody gave me."

He studied me for a moment and said, "Must be some sad poems by the way you're looking. Your eyes are red, you feeling all right?" When I made no further comment, he looked at the front door and said, "Is Feen here?"

"She sure is. She is inside cooking breakfast. Do you want to eat?"

"I sure do. I guess I got here just in time."

Mom heard us, and came on the porch laughing. "Hey, Adrian," she exclaimed. "Come on in yer 'n git some grits, eggs and sausage. Haven't seen ya since March. How ya son doin'?" I couldn't help but smile as I watched the two of them together.

Her face lit up with a smile when she looked at him and vice versa.

"He's doing fine. Graduating high school next year."

"Dat is good news. Graduating, huh? Dat mean you good at somethin'," she laughed. "What wife you with now?"

He laughed. "Wow, Feen, you really know how to knock a fella in the gut. I'm presently alone, just like I told you last time. I intend to stay that way. If I happen to marry somebody, I promise, you will be the first to know. So, will you please stop asking me that?" He continued laughing, knowing she wouldn't.

Then it came to me. I thought about what Adrian had said last year about me being able to count on him and what Delores had said about him being a good catch. Looking at him now, I could see that he was. I need to get married and whom else can I ask to do me that favor, but Adrian. The man who has been there to help my family and me and not ask for anything in return, really, except kindness, respect and acceptance.

I followed my mother and Adrian into our small light pink wallpapered kitchen, where the aroma of breakfast floated, and my stomach started to do somersaults, but somehow everything stayed down. I was determined to sit and talk to them without getting nauseated. A refrigerator and stove occupied one wall. Angie was washing dishes at the sink right by the backdoor.

Since the table was against the wall, usually only three people could sit at it and Adrian sat at one end and I sat at the other end. My mom stood at the stove cooking breakfast.

"How are your Mom and Dad doing? I don't get out in that direction very often," I said.

Adrian answered, "They're fine. Daddy still pretends to be a farmer. He keeps a large garden. He grows some of the sweetest tasting tomatoes on this earth. Mom cans everything they can't eat. Since it's just the two of 'em, there's a lot. Ran out of space in the house, so Dad and I built her a little house in the backyard. I fuss at 'em for all they do, but I'm glad they have something to do they like."

"Ya right," Mom said. "Ah hope I'm lucky 'nuf to be busy lack dat when I'm they age. Ah tell ya, it's a blessin'."

"How long are you going to be here?" I asked.

"About two weeks. Why? What do you need me to do for you?" Adrian asked with a wide grin.

"Well," I said hesitantly, "I have a little project for you, but I can't tell you about it now. Can you come back by tomorrow?" I asked.

He drew together his brow and said, "Well, I'll have to check my schedule." Then burst into laughter. "I'm just kidding. I can come back by tomorrow. But, why can't you tell me about it now?"

"I have some details to work out first. Please say that you will come by tomorrow."

"Ok, you know that I can never say no to any of you ladies. What time?"

"About five p.m. We'll be back from church by then."

My mother was busy preparing the food, and I could feel her eyes on me. We sat around the table, ate and joked around like people who know each other well.

When Adrian was leaving, he looked at me, opened his mouth and then thought better of it. I have to wait until tomorrow to make sure in my heart and mind this is what I wanted to do.

"You be careful," I said.

"You too, and I will see you both tomorrow," he said as he got into his car and drove away.

"Char, what dis 'bout? Why ya wanna talk ta Adrian?"

"I'll tell you after I talk with him, I promise."

She walked away, but for the rest of the night, I'd see her watch me off and on.

I have to find a solution before I discussed it with her, I thought. She has been through enough. She has to take care of

Angie and she is worried about Laura's situation. I am a grown, educated woman, with a job. I can stand on my own two feet.

That night as I lay in my bed in the room I shared with my sister, Angie, I watched her as she slept soundly in her bunk bed. I felt strangely removed from these surroundings. I looked at the lace curtains on the window, which was my feeble attempt to create whimsy and feminine softness, in an otherwise bleak room with walls of unpainted lumber. I tried to plan how I was going to ask Adrian to be my husband.

I had been so focused on my pregnancy that I had not thought about that I was going to be a mother. My heart pounded as I thought about having a baby. Knowing that I may have a solution to my problem afforded me the opportunity for the first time, to think about and be glad about this child I was bringing into the world. Someone to love, guide and protect.

CHAPTER 9

*Y*ou gonna wear a hole in the flow the way ya walkin' back and forf," Mom said as she stirred batter to bake a cake.

"Just a little anxious, that's all," I said. I'd changed into a casual skirt and blouse and sat on the porch and waited.

Adrian arrived at five o'clock. He was dressed in black slacks and a crisp blue shirt. I normally did not notice how he dressed, but I guess because I had begun to think of him as my future husband, I was aware of how he presented himself. After all, I wanted to be proud of my husband.

He smiled at me and said, "What's going on, Girl?"

"Just waiting for you," I said, not meeting his eyes.

As my mother came to the door, I grabbed my purse and stepped down the steps. She said, "I sho' wish I knew what goin' on in dat head of yourn. But Adrian, take care of 'er."

"Sure thing. You know I'll do that," he said.

Neither one of us said a word as he drove to CB's Cafe. I looked out of the window and fidgeted with my purse.

"I know it's early, but I thought we might have some chow while we talked. I have to say, you really got me wondering what in the world you want to talk to me about. I have racked my brains trying to figure out if I did something wrong to you."

"No, no. It's nothing like that. Yes, I think it's a good idea to eat while we talk."

∞

My heartbeat was so loud, it sounded like drum rolls in my head. The waitress asked, "Would you two like to have something to drink before you eat?"

"I'll just have a cream soda" I replied. I really wanted to have a glass of wine, but because of the baby, I knew it was best if I did not have any alcoholic beverages. "I need something to bolster my nerves, but a cream soda will have to do," I said.

Adrian raised his eyebrows at my last remark. I'm sure he wandered what I needed to talk to him about that I would need to bolster my nerves. After we ordered dinner, he tapped his hand on the table three times and said, "Well, let's have it. I don't think I can stand another minute without knowing what in the world is going on with you?"

As I gazed into his curious eyes, all of my best-laid plans went out of the window and I decided to just tell him the truth. "Adrian, I am in a tight spot and I know this is asking a lot of you, because it would mean you would have to give up your life for a little while."

His eyebrows knotted up. "What do you mean, give up my life? What kind of spot are you in that would cause me to give up my life?"

"I'm pregnant," I said.

I took a deep breath and exhaled. It's finally out, I thought. Someone besides me now knows this horrible and wonderful secret. "And when my principal finds out, I will be fired. Besides that, I will be humiliated and disgraced."

"Pregnant, are you serious?" He dimmed his eyes and clenched his teeth.

I said seriously, "Yes, I am. I am two months pregnant."

"Two months?" he said as he lay back in his seat. "That's all. You may be having a false alarm."

"No. I am not having a false alarm. I have been having morning sickness. I'm a month late and I'm never this late. I may be late for a week, but not a month. I know I am pregnant."

"Maybe, he won't fire you. Maybe, he'll just suspend you until next year, after you have the baby."

"No, he is going to fire me. That's what he did with Miss Allen last year. She got pregnant and he fired her on the spot, the day he found out and she wasn't even showing yet. It's part of the morals clause that teachers sign when they're hired," I said.

All of the pent up emotions of the past few months flowed out of me. I could feel some of the jittery feelings subside. It felt good to tell it to somebody.

"Do you know how hard my mother worked to put me through college? Do you know during that time even with all she was doing, there were still months I could not buy a meal book and walked around Grambling's campus hungry?"

"Yeah," he said. "I know. You wrote to me some of those times and I did what I could to help."

"Yeah, you did and I thank you so very much for that. There were months I ate honey buns and potato chips for my meals for breakfast, dinner and supper. There were times when the soles of my shoes got holes in them and I put cardboard in the bottom," I said. "I just want you to understand how hard it was for me to make it through college. But I did, I made it through."

He sat in silence and did not take his eyes away from me. I could not tell what he thought about me or my pregnancy.

"I am holding a lot of hopes and dreams for my mother. She did not have the education or the opportunity to go to college and she is just so proud of Laura and me, finishing school and having jobs other than being a maid or picking cotton. All of that is for nothing. All of that is gone," I emphasized. "If I get fired, there is no other professional job here for me. I will have to leave the state and take tests in another state to get certified to teach. Do you understand what I am saying?" I emphasized.

In a whisper that I could barely get out, "I have to get married."

"Who is the father?" he asked, with his eyes squinted. "I didn't know you were dating anyone."

I took a deep breath and started to cry. I had done a lot of crying, since I realized I was probably pregnant, but I was still not cried out. Now it flowed. People at other tables watched us. I guess they thought Adrian had hurt me in some way, because they eyed him hostilely. I excused myself from the table and went to the bathroom. I didn't come back until I'd composed myself.

He said, "Does Feen know?"

I shook my head. "No, I have been hiding my morning sickness from her, which is a hard thing to do in a small house. I didn't want to tell her until I knew what I was going to do," I said.

"Who is the father?" he repeated.

"Ray Dean, a teacher at my school. He's married," I choked. I started to cry again.

"Oh my Lord," said Adrian. "What do you want me to do? Beat him up, get a shotgun and make him marry you. Whatever you want, I'm game."

"I want you to marry me," I whispered, afraid to look at him.

His eyes got big. "What?"

"Just until I have the baby. Then we can get a divorce. It's okay to get a divorce and be a teacher, but it's not okay to have a baby out of wedlock," I said. "So, we could get married, have the baby and then we can get a divorce."

"Oh boy," he said. "Do you know what you're asking? Girl, I

have been married three times. I am not husband material. Marriage is a dirty word in my dictionary. 'Sides you don't want no old codger like me."

"Adrian, this is different. We're not really going to be married. We'll just be pretending. I am not going to be demanding anything from you but your name and for you to not run around on me, for appearances sake, until we're divorced."

Our eyes met and I said, "That is not a long time to be faithful."

"What about this guy, Dean Ray? How do you feel about him, and does he know about the baby?" he asked.

"Ray Dean," I corrected.

"What?"

"Ray Dean, you said Dean Ray. I was correcting you on his name."

"I don't care what his name is. Answer my questions. How do you feel about him, and does he know about the baby?" he queried with a stern look.

"I don't know how I feel about him. I know when I realized I was pregnant, my solution to the problem did not include him. No, I have not shared this information with him and I'm not sure I will," I said.

"What do you mean by your solution to the problem did not include him? You and he did the do and made the problem. I know how a man thinks. I'm not in the market for getting shot."

"Like I said, he's married. So trying to get together with him would cause more problems. There is no way he could get a divorce and marry me before I started to show. Even if he wanted to. I'm not sure he would want to." I felt myself on the edge of tears again.

"I see what you mean," he said thoughtfully. "Ok. When did the doctor say this baby is due?"

"I have not been to a doctor yet, because I did not want to see a doctor in Marksville. Somehow, the word might get out that I'm pregnant. I need to set up an appointment in Alexandria."

"I repeat, you may not even be pregnant," he said.

"The way I've been throwing up, I'm pregnant. I will set up an appointment in Alexandria and you can come with me. Will you do that?" I asked.

He thought for a moment and said, "Okay, I'm not gonna let you go through this alone." Then after a moment, he asked, "Whatcha going to tell Feen? I want her to know the truth. I don't want her to think I ever took advantage of you. Can we agree on that?"

I said, "Yes, indeed. Of course, I will come clean to Mom about all the details. I just wanted to have some kind of solution before I talked to her, that's all. She doesn't need another problem she'll have to solve. Then you'll do it?" I asked excitedly.

"We need to find out if you're pregnant or not. Then we will meet with your mother and tell her everything. If she's okay with it, then we will let everyone know, my parents first."

"Ok, that sounds good," I said. "There aren't enough words to tell you how grateful I am."

Sitting in the little café across from Adrian, the drums in my head quieted and I could actually taste my food, and my stomach flutters eased. I wanted to jump up and down in happiness. He not only agreed to do it, but he agreed to help me plan the best way to get this done so there would be little suspicion.

CHAPTER 10

I lay on a cold table with my legs up in stirrups. This was a new experience for me. I had never been undressed in front of man, who wasn't my boyfriend before, let along lie half naked with my behind exposed. A sobering experience, indeed. A nurse stood behind the doctor as he examined me. His instruments were cold and invasive. I closed my eyes tight and waited for this humiliation to be over. When I opened my eyes, the nurse smiled reassuringly at me. I attempted to smile back. Not sure I made it all the way. A gloved hand invaded me and I fervently hoped this would end soon.

"You're pregnant and you're due in April," the doctor said and confirmed my suspicions.

When I stepped into the waiting room, and saw Adrian as he sat, the relief I felt was overwhelming. It must be how the swallows felt when they return to Capistrano in the Spring. I ran into his arms and he said, "I guess this means you were right. We'll get through this. Where do you want to go?"

"Turner's Department store. I need to buy three dresses, for me, Mom and Angie."

I went about it very methodically. I wanted something nice, but not too expensive. It was going to be a private ceremony. I picked out three party dresses. Mine was a white short sleeve dress, with a pencil skirt and scooped neckline. It was overlaid with lace and stopped at my knees. Angie's and Mom's were the same, only theirs were pastel blue. As I touched the fabric of the dresses, I grasped the realization: this was my actual bridal and wedding party ensembles. For a moment, my heart shrunk. Nothing about this was how I'd dreamed picking my bridal ensemble would be. I put those thoughts away. I have to deal with the situation at hand. Adrian sat in the store, but I did not ask his opinion on the dresses I'd picked. After all, he was a pretend husband and although we were going to be making a lot of decisions together, discussing dresses with him might make it too real. We wanted to keep it in the pretend mode. It would be easier that way.

So now the next job on my list was to inform my mother. This was not a job I was looking forward to, but it had to be done. She had been curious since Saturday, but had not pushed me for information. I'd caught her looking at me as if she was trying to figure it out. I think she sensed this was serious enough that I would have to tell her some time. We arrived at Dr. Frank's house and waited for her. Her face was expressionless when she saw Adrian. It was as if Adrian came with me to pick her up everyday.

"Hi Mom," I said.

"How do," she replied. "Y'all together today?"

"Yes, we were, Mom. I will explain everything to you today. I promise. Let's wait until we get home so we can talk face to face."

"All right." she said. "Ah kin wait 'til we git home. I waited dis long."

No one said anything else until we got home and sat at the kitchen table.

"Okay, Charlawt, whatcha need ta talk ta Adrian 'bout?" Mom

asked.

My pulse raced and I felt dizzy. Finally, I choked out the words. "Mom, I'm pregnant."

For a minute, her face didn't change. Then the clouds came. Her eyebrows came together and her body stiffened.

"Whatcha say? You're gonna haf a baby?" She shook her head from side to side in disbelief. "Knowed somethin' was wrong. Da way ya been sittin' on de garry by ya self. Don't eat nothin'. Time I fix something', run outside on de garry. Lawd, haf mercy."

"I'm so sorry," I said.

When Angie heard the commotion, she ran out of her room, "What's wrong, Mom?"

"Angie, please, go back to your room," I said. "I'll tell you about it later." She continued to stare at Mom. "Angie, go to your room," I repeated more forcefully. The house was so small she would still hear everything, but at least she wouldn't be underfoot.

Mom sat there shaking her head, looking off in the distance. Angie turned and went back into her room.

Adrian reached over and patted her on the hands. After a while, she said, "Is it fur dat snake, Ray Dean?"

I nodded my head. "Yes."

She hit her fist on the table, "Dammit, Ah tole, ya Charlawt. Ah seen de signs. Didn't wanta believe it. Not my girl," Mom continued, as though we weren't in the room. "Brought ya up better'n dat."

Her words stung. "I really messed up. I should have listened to you. I didn't see it coming." I sobbed.

"Whatcha mean ya didn't see it coming," she said, in a high shrieking voice, staring me down. "Dis ain't de firs' time he got a girl in de fam'ly way. But he Professor Pearson bruh-n-law. Dat why he not fired dat time. But Ah saw it coming and Ah tole ya, Charlawt. Ya lie with dogs, ya get flees. Haven't Ah tole ya dat? Answer me. Answer me." She burst into deep jerking tears that shook her whole body with each sob and her hands flew up to her face. Adrian rose, pulled her into his arms and rocked her back and forth. My mom did not cry easily. Over the years, except for when my father left, I had not seen her cry. My soul ached for the pain I'd caused her. This is why I had been so hesitant to tell her.

"Yes, Mom, you told me."

After what seemed like forever, she calmed down and sat back down in her chair. Her head jerked toward Adrian, who had also sat back down, and her eyes met his.

"So, why you wanta talk ta Adrian?" she asked still looking at him, then turned her scrutiny to me. "He a friend of Ray Dean?" She was calmer, but her voice was still hard and her words deliberate.

"You know what happened to the last teacher that got pregnant. So, I'm going to get fired, unless I can get married."

Mom waited for a few seconds before she answered, "Yeah, Ah 'member when dat chile got pregnant 'n she weren't marr'd. Yeah, he fired 'er. What dat got ta do with Adrian?"

"I wanted to talk to Adrian because I need to get married. Adrian and I can get married and then get divorced after the baby is born," I said.

Her mouth and eyes opened wide and her head turned swiftly toward Adrian. She stared at him for a while and he looked back at her with his brows up as if he's waiting for her consent. Then she turned back to me.

"What? What? Mus' be out of your mind?" Her voice shrieked.

"No, Mom. It could work. Listen to me, please, Mom."

"You selfish chile. What 'bout Adrian? Ah know he don't tell us 'bout 'em, but I'm sho' Adrian has women in Texas. Is he 'spose ta give 'em up fur ya? He gonna leave his job in Texas? Ya gonna tell ya baby who his daddy is or ya gonna tell 'im, it Adrian? Where y'all gonna stay?"

Adrian said, "Well, I can answer some of those. I do not have any girlfriends waiting that will cause problems and I'll find something I can do on my own here. Since we gonna get a divorce, we're not gonna sleep in the same bed or have sex. We don't have a place to stay, so I'll start looking tomorrow."

"Adrian, ya know I trust you," said Mom. "Dis my li'l girl 'n Ah don't wanna see 'er hurt. Or you hurt either, fur dat matt'r. Ya my bes' friend."

"I know that," said Adrian as he nodded his head. "Feen, come outside with me a minute," he said. She stood up but did not move. "Please."

"Okay," she said and then followed him outside.

I could not hear what they said, but I could see their body language. The conversation seemed intense. One talked and the other listened, and vice versa. They went on for about fifteen minutes before they came back inside of the house.

My mom trudged into the house with rounded shoulders, instead of shoulders back as she usually walked. She folded her arms, and did not meet my eyes. She said, "Fine. If dis what ya need to do, then do it."

"I'm right here, you two," addressing both of them, but looking at Adrian. "I'm grown and," looking at Mom, "Mom, those are some legitimate questions you posed and we will discuss all of them. But we don't have a lot of time to argue about it, we have to get married soon."

"Alright," she said. "Alright," she repeated. "Jes' tell me if'n ya need something. Ah can't stan' too much mo' of dis. I'm goin' ta bed."

I heard her say under her breath, "Ya don' listen ta me no way. If ya did, wouldn't be in dis mess."

She looked absolutely beaten as she went into her room.

Adrian whispered, "Don't worry, Charlotte, she'll be all right. She's a strong woman. She gets through what she's gotta get through."

"I think she'll be all right, once she sees her grandbaby. But I feel like the world has been lifted off of me, just telling her has made me feel so much lighter."

∞

On Wednesday, when I picked up my mother at Dr. Frank's house, she seemed distracted. I asked her what was wrong. She told me the doctor's yardman, Joe, had a heart attack that day and died. We knew him well. He even attended our church. Finding this out was sad.

Later on that evening, while driving to his parents' house, I told Adrian that Joe had died.

"Sorry to hear that," said Adrian. "Does he still do Dr. Frank's yard?"

"Yes, he does," I said. "That's how I found out about it today from Mom."

"Do you think Feen would ask Dr. Frank if he'd give me a chance to do his yard?"

"What?" I said. "Are you serious? Do you really want me to ask my mother to talk to Dr. Frank for you?"

"Yes, I am serious," he said. "If I can get Dr. Frank's yard to mow and trim, and then get some of the other yards in that neighborhood, I could supplement my pension and be my own boss. Set my own schedule."

"Sure, I'll ask her," I said. "I'll ask her when I get home tonight. I don't think she will have a problem doing that."

Adrian's Mom's was short and a little plump. She almost always wore an apron, except for church. Her long gray straight hair was styled in a long braid that was wrapped around the circumference of her head. Mr. Fonteneau was tall and built with the same slim frame as Adrian. They were both very light complexioned. They greeted us warmly when we arrived at his childhood home. I'd known Adrian's parents all of my life. Consequently, I was not nervous to meet with them. A nice evening breeze blew as we drank ice tea on the large porch, and we told them about our plan to marry.

Exchanging glances with his father, his mother said, "Well, I'm surprised. We always thought he hung 'round Feen's house 'cuz he lacked Feen. It couldn't been you, cuz you were too li'l. But, we glad 'bout it. Just surprised, s'all. Do you know what you're getting into?" she asked.

I got a heavy feeling in my heart after I heard Adrian's mother's remarks. Even though I knew some of my mother's friends thought that, I never thought of Mom and Adrian as a couple. In all of the time he'd visited us, I'd never noticed anything romantic between them. In fact, I'd always thought of Adrian as sort of an uncle, and as a younger brother to my mother? However, Adrian did not seem to be at all surprised by that revelation.

"Yes, ma'am, I know what I'm getting into. We love each other very much," I said. Well, that wasn't a lie, I thought. We do love each other. We're just not in love with each other.

At the last part, Adrian's eyes turned towards me and he smiled.

He said, "Mom, I told you, many times before, I have always felt bad about Lucien abandoning his family. I felt like I should take his place and do whatever I could for them."

"Well," she patted me on my hand, smiled and said, "I always wanted a schoolteacher in the fam'ly, and now we'll have one, and such a pretty one too." Then her eyes went to Adrian, "A parent wants her child to have someone they can share their life with. I know you and Feen are good and fine people, and you will make my son a fine wife."

I hugged her, "Thank you so much. I'll do my best to make

him happy."

We had a slice of cake to go with the tea before we left. I took a deep breath and savored the moment. I did feel a tinge of guilt because they would be disappointed when we would get a divorce, but we would cross that bridge when we got to it.

It was about eight thirty p.m. when Adrian dropped me off at home. Mom sitting in the living room watching television. She didn't look up or acknowledge me when I walked in.

I wondered if she was still upset with me. "What's wrong, Mom?" I asked.

"Called Laura taday. Say she fine, but Ah don't believe 'er."

"Why don't you believe her?" I asked.

"Not sho'. Somethin' 'bout 'er voice," she said. "Bay, I'm jes so worried 'bout 'er."

"Mom, I understand what you're saying. I am too. But it does no good for us to worry. We're doing all that we can do. You called her and she said she was okay."

"Ah know." She looked up at me and said. "Are ya doin' ok? Ya know ya wit' chile, so don't ov'rdo."

"I know Mom. I know. I am being careful."

"Mom," I said. "Will you recommend Adrian to be Joe's replacement as his yardman to Dr. Frank?"

"What?" asked my mother. She stood up, put her hands on her hips and just starred at me.

I told her about Adrian's plans to cut yards and build his own business.

Feen continued to be surprised. "Hmm. Well, dat a good idea. Adrian taking dis serious. Retirement and yard work money. Good thinkin'. Want ta do right by ya. Yeah, I'll talk ta Miss Frank, she the one does the hirin' of the yardmen and anyone else dat works 'roun de house. I'll let ya know."

She nodded her head up and down, turned and walked into the kitchen. I heard her as she sung a Negro spiritual "Lord Thank

You." I could see she was wondering if this might, indeed, be the solution to the predicament I had gotten myself into.

∞

On Thursday, when I informed Delores, and some of the other teachers, about my plans to get married, the expressions on their faces were ones of open mouths, wide eyes and raised eyebrows. After all, I had not even mentioned dating anyone, much less, thinking about marrying someone. But, I had walked around school with a smile pasted to my face all day and I think my mood convinced them. Therefore, after a minute or two, everyone recovered and they smiled and shook my hand and patted me on the shoulders. The ladies asked about a ring and with the suddenness of everything, I had forgotten all about a ring. I said he wanted me to pick it out and we would shop for a ring that Saturday.

By the end of the day, word of my pending nuptials had gotten around school, and I looked up as Ray approached me. He had a very serious frown on his face. This was not a scene I was looking forward to. He said, "Charlotte, what in the hell is going on? I heard you are getting married."

"Hi, Ray. How have you been? I've been fine. I guess you wouldn't know that, since you haven't bothered to call me since July Fourth," I replied.

"Is it true?" he asked.

"Yes, it is," I replied as I threw my chin up in the air.

"Why would you do that?"

"Why wouldn't I do that?"

He stared me down with his legs apart like he was ready to go into battle.

"Because I love him," I said. "We want to be together. We want to spend the rest of our lives together." Internal warmth radiated throughout my body. It felt good as I told him these things. For the first time, I realized how angry I was with him. How he had not made any attempt to see or talk to me or even ask about how I've been. If what I said was going to hurt him, then I wanted to do that.

"I don't understand you," he said. "I know you and you have never even mentioned this guy. Now, all of a sudden, you're getting married? Think about what you're doing, Charlotte. I can tell you, marrying a person you don't love just to be married will end up hurting you both," he said desperately. He reached out to put his hand on my arm and I jumped as if I had touched a hot stove.

"What. What. What," I repeated. "What do you want from me?"

"You know how I feel about you," he said.

"I know no such thing," I answered. "No such thing. You are a married man. There is no future for us. I need to know whatever I feel for someone, they feel the same way about me. Adrian loves me and I love him. Now, I have to go. I have some errands to run before I pick up my mother."

"I don't know what's happening. I know you don't love this guy. I feel the electricity in the space between us right now. Please, think about what you're doing. I know I don't have the right to ask you anything, but please think about it," he ended and walked away and I watched as he did so.

He was right, there was still something between us, and I didn't know if I would get over it. But, I did know I would stay faithful to my marriage vows. I'd asked Adrian to do that and I would have to do it also.

I exhaled and let go of what might have been, but will never be.

∞

"Char, I was thinking, maybe, we don't need to get a house together," Adrian said. We were sitting in his car in front of my house, after work. He had come to pick me up to look at houses to rent.

"What you mean?" I asked.

"Well, you could stay at your mom's and I could stay at mine until the divorce."

"What? No way."

"Why not?"

"Because everyone will know something is wrong. They'll know the marriage is fake when I turn up pregnant and we're not even living together."

"What does that matter? You'll be married, so Professor Pearson can't fire you. Isn't that what you want?"

"Yes, that's what I want, but I also want to make sure everyone believes it's your baby."

"Oh, I see," he said thoughtfully. "Well, I have three prospects. One is near your mom's. The other is with my mom and the last is a little house out in Hickory Hill."

"Near my mom's, you mean the old Kirby house? Uh uh. No, I don't want to live that close. What do you mean by with your mom?"

"Just that. Mom and Dad have two extra rooms and they have offered for us to stay there for a while."

"Well, if we stay there, we'll have to sleep in separate beds and then they will know something is wrong and if we sleep in the same bed, well, I don't know." I looked away. I felt heat around my neck.

He laid his head back on his seat, and closed his eyes. I felt my stomach go queasy. Was this too much for him to do? Had he decided to back out?

"Adrian, what's wrong? If it's the money, you know that I

work. I'll help with the bills," I said.

"No, it's not that. You seemed to be all tied up about what people think about you. Do you realize that a lot of people are going to think I am marrying someone young enough to be my daughter? What do you think they're going to think about me? Should I be worried about that? It doesn't seem to bother you about that."

I folded my arms and starred at the pecan tree in our yard. I felt tears behind my eyes and I fought to hold them back. "I'm sorry. You're right. I have been focused on my problem. I have not looked at it from your perspective. That's because I don't think of you like that. I mean about your age. To me you're just Adrian. No labels. Just Adrian. Please, forgive me. Look, if it matters that much to you, we can live wherever you want us to."

The silence stretched on for what seemed an eternity, but it was actually less than a minute.

"Okay," he said. "Let's go look at the house in Hickory Hill."

The house was a white wood frame house with a big front yard, a porch that was surrounded by shrubs, a paved driveway and a large backyard. The owner was standing in the yard waiting for us. He opened the door for us and he allowed us to walk around inside on our own.

It was an older home that had been remodeled and was in good shape. It had two bedrooms, one bathroom, living room, and dining area that connected to the kitchen. Also, in the kitchen was a washer. A clothesline in the back yard to hang my clothes out to dry completed the picture.

Adrian said, "What do you think?"

I beamed and said, "It's perfect. It is absolutely perfect."

I walked around with a huge smile on my face. I felt giddy and I pinched myself.

Adrian said, "Char, what in the world are you doing?"

"I'm pinching myself. I can hardly believe this is going to be mine. You know I love living with Mom and eating her cooking, but a grown person likes to be on their own. With my small salary, I couldn't figure a way to make this happen."

"Yeah, I know. Will you be able to afford it later? You know, after the divorce."

"I think so. All of the startup costs will already have been paid. So, I should be able to handle the rest. I want to hug you. Can I hug you?"

"You sure can. In fact, I insist on it."

He laughed as his arms enfolded me. He picked me up off of the ground and turned me around in a circle before he put me down.

We joined the owner in the yard. I'd walked to a side section of the yard where my mind envisioned a flowerbed, when I noticed a car coming slowly down the road. This road had a few houses scattered along it, and had hardly any pass-through traffic. Anyone on this road is going to a particular place. My heart beat hard in my chest, because it looked like Ray's car. The car sped up and I could not see who was in it. I turned to see if Adrian had noticed, but he was deep in conversation with the owner. I was perplexed. What was he doing down here? He lived in town. I am going to ask him when I see him, I thought.

∞

On Friday, Adrian sat on my front porch with a small gift-wrapped package in his hand. My heart was in my throat, because it looked like a small jewelry box, and we had decided that I would pick out my ring myself. Yet, here he was with a ring he had chosen. I held my breath.

"Char, I have a gift for you," he said.

I took the gift and unwrapped it and indeed, it was a jewelry box. I slowly opened the box and inside was a ring. Even to my untrained eyes, I could see the stone was glass and the band was large and not made of gold. "Oh," I said. I could feel his eyes on me.

"Aw," he said, "You don't like it?"

I opened my mouth and nothing came out. I searched my brain for something to say and nothing came. I did not want to hurt his feelings. The ring sat in my hand as I continued to stare at it. Finally, I elevated my eyes to his face and he moved around in the seat across from me with his eyebrows raised. "It's not that I don't like it, but where can I wear it?"

"You don't like it," he repeated in a sad voice, as he looked down at the floor.

"But, I thought we were going to pick out the rings today."

"Yeah, I know. But I thought about it last night and I decided with the cost of renting a house and everything, we could save some money on the rings. I mean, after all, what do you do with an engagement ring after the divorce?"

"Adrian, I'm not crazy. I wasn't going to pick out a high-priced ring. I care too much about you to waste your money, but I did want it to be real."

He pointed at the ring. "That ring is real and it's not high priced."

"We need a ring to make the marriage look legitimate."

"There you go again, worried about what people are going to think."

I got up, because I could no longer sit. Something inside of me needed to move around. My eyes surveyed the road, the trees, and the pasture across the road and nowhere could I find an answer to solve this problem. "Okay," I said. "I can wear it for the ceremony, but I won't be able to wear it otherwise, because it will turn my finger green." I continued to look across the road, when I heard a small sound coming from Adrian. He sat with his hand over his mouth as he tried to conceal a big grin. It started with a giggle and grew into full-blown laughter. He laughed so hard until he bent in two and hugged his stomach.

"What are you laughing at?" I asked.

He continued to laugh and could not answer. Finally, he said, "Your face, when you saw that ring." At which time, he laughed anew.

"Why is that funny?" I looked at him in amazement.

"I can't explain it to you. You would have to see it. I bought a costume jewelry ring from the Five and Dime Store and put it in one of my mom's old ring boxes. The look on your face was worth all of the trouble."

"You mean you're not serious about this being my ring."

"Of course not. I would never do that to you."

"I can't believe you played a joke on me like that."

"Sorry Char, you know me, just having a little fun." They sat silent for a moment. "Do you think you will enjoy living with me?"

I shook my head and said, "I don't know. I really don't know. I hope you can take it as well as you can dish it out."

"We'll see," he said. "Let's go."

We bought our marriage license and visited several furniture stores in Alexandria and we ended up at a jewelry store in the Alexandria Shopping Center, where we picked out rings.

As I entered the jewelry store, my stomach turned over and I imagined how I'd feel if I were actually here to purchase a ring for a "real marriage" and not a "pretend marriage." What if Ray were here with me instead of Adrian?

"Well, Char, do you see anything you like?" Adrian asked.

"Not yet," I replied.

Adrian stood near the door as I walked around the glass counters and looked at the rings. Shiny bands of gold and light that hit prisms just right made for a tinkling experience. Finally, I saw the perfect set. A set that was stunning, yet the stone was small. I pointed to the set and the clerk retrieved it from the counter. I tried it on as Adrian approached. We both beheld the ring and smiled.

I said, "This is it."

Adrian said, "This is quite a bit different than your first ring."

"Don't remind me of that. I told you that I wouldn't be extravagant," I said.

"That you did."

"Where is the matching male wedding band?" I asked the clerk.

"No," said Adrian. "I don't need that."

"I'll buy it," I said.

"It's not that." He stopped rubbed his chin. "When I put a ring on my finger, I want it to mean something, you know."

"It does mean something. It's my gift to you to celebrate our relationship. Okay?"

He closed his eyes, exhaled and nodded. "Okay."

"I have a nice wedding band that will go wonderfully with your set," said the clerk.

He took out a simple gold male band and presented it to us.

"What do you think?" I asked.

Adrian said, "That's it. That will work."

We bought the three rings and Adrian gave them to me for safekeeping. As he drove back to Marksville, he looked across at me and said, "Well, Char, this has been quite a week. We got a lot done."

"Yes, we did," I said. "Where there's a will, there's a way. You know, we make a good team."

"Yes, we do," he said.

For a moment, I had a flashback about the Christmas program when I'd said the same thing about Ray. But then, I shrugged it off and concentrated on this team of Adrian and me. Tomorrow we would begin a new chapter in our lives.

CHAPTER 11

Today was my wedding day. I felt tingly all over. We were to be at my pastor's house at ten o'clock a.m. for the ceremony. The three of us got dressed and my mother asked me, "Do ya haf' somethin' old, somethin' new, somethin' borrow, somethin' blue?"

I said, "Mom, I'm not worried about that. This is not for real, remember?"

"Dis is ya weddin' day. Dis might not be ya only weddin' day, but it is ya weddin' day. Wan' it ta be right," she said.

Something had been on my mind since we told Adrian's parents we were getting married. The way she had insinuated there might be something between Mom and Adrian. I'd also heard the same thing whispered when I told my mother's friends who worked in the school lunchroom. I hoped that to fulfill my desire to keep my job and avoid dishonor, I had not destroyed my Mom's chance at the happiness she deserved.

I took a deep breath, and forged forward, "Mom, am I doing the right thing? I mean, am I coming between you and Adrian? Was there something romantic between the two of you?"

At first, my mother looked at me with a frown and tilted her head to the side. Then, she smiled, but it did not reach her eyes, and said, "Oh, my baby, No. Ya not comin' between Adrian 'n me." She pulled me into her arms for a moment. "Adrian been a 'rock in a weary land' ta me. I admit dat. He he'p me at a time I really need it. 'Sides dat, I jes lack talkin' ta 'im. He make me laugh. Adrian been all ov'r de world in de service and I lack hearing 'bout places I ain't never been," she finished.

"But I have heard several people mention since I revealed my intentions to marry him, they thought he came around here because he was interested in you. I never thought of it that way. But I was a child and maybe, just didn't notice. So, I just wanted to make sure this was all right with you, and wasn't going to affect your hopes and dreams."

"Bay, whatcha wan' me ta say? He been dere fur me in my darkes' hour."

"You mean when Dad left?"

She hesitated, then said, "Dat's one of de times. Maybe if he wasn' too youn' fur me, somethin' mighta happen. We ain't n'evr be tageth'r. Ya know, lack a man and woman. I swear, no matter wha' folk say. Believe dat," she said as she examined my face.

"You think people will say I'm too young for him?" I asked.

"Some folk will. All 'n all, folk look at thin' diff'rent fur a man. They dun thin' nothin' 'bout n older man wid a youn' woman. Anyway, ya need him now 'n he wanta he'p ya. Dun worry 'bout me. I'm happy if my chil'ren happy. Now let's see if we got dose thin' ya need to haf.'"

I still didn't really understand their relationship. Her answers only confused me more. But she said it's okay, and I don't have any other option.

"Well, my dress is new," I said.

Angie said as she entered the room, "I have the pearl earrings you and Laura gave me for Christmas. Would you like to borrow those?"

"Ok, thank you Angie. I love you, Girl," I smiled. "I got a blue evening purse."

"Somethin' old," Mom said and then repeated, "somethin' old." She stood with her hands on her hips and looked up to the right. "Yer' my blue han'kerchief, dat'll match ya blue purse an' it old."

I hugged my mom and said, "You are the absolute best."

This was not the way I had dreamed my wedding would be. I had dreamed of a long white gown, six bridesmaids, a flower girl, a church filled with flowers and a huge reception afterwards in my mom's backyard. Then my groom and I would go on a fabulous honeymoon. We would be passionately in love and we would make love all night long.

Although I wasn't in love with Adrian, I did love him. I thought of him and that cheap ring stunt he'd pulled and smiled to myself. I could not ask for a better partner to go through this difficult time with.

We completed getting dressed and soon we were at the pastor's house.

"My, my, you look handsome," I said when I saw my groom. He stood before me in a black suit, with one hand in his pocket, revealing a starched white shirt, and a gold tie. His lean face exposed his high cheekbones, with straight eyebrows and evenly set eyes. His thick mustache was freshly trimmed over a wide mouth and brilliant white teeth. His brown curly hair begged for fingers to run through it. The lopsided smile he gave me let me know he knew how good he looked and my heart actually skipped a beat.

"Thank you, Ma'am," he answered. Dimming his eyes, he said, "And you are absolutely stunning."

"Thank you," I said, unable to meet his eyes. Adrian took my hand in his and put his other hand under my chin so we were eye to eye and said, "Char, are you sure that you want to do this? It's not too late to back out?"

I nodded my head and said, "Yes, yes I do. I appreciate so much your offering to not do this after all the money we have already spent, but I am ready."

He chuckled and said, "Going once, going twice, gone."

We walked into the pastor's home and I felt strangely at peace. It wasn't until the pastor's wife played "Lead Me, Guide Me," that I wondered if I was doing the right thing. I took a sideways glance at Adrian, but I could not tell what he was thinking. He looked fine. Then the vows began and my heart beat hard in my chest, so hard I could barely hear what the pastor said. Somehow, I answered when I was supposed to. By the time, we exchanged rings, my heart settled down and my hearing returned to normal.

"With this ring I thee wed, and all my worldly goods I thee endow. In sickness and in health, in poverty or in wealth, 'til death do us part."

My throat felt dry. "I do," I answered.

When Adrian said, "I do," my heart was full and I felt tears come into my eyes.

The pastor said, "Kiss the bride." Adrian smiled, leaned forward and gave me a light peck on the lips, followed by a big hug. My heart jumped in my chest again, and then heaviness in my stomach at the brief kiss. I reminded myself this was pretend. Hence, he'd given me a very sterile kiss.

I looked over at my mother and she sobbed. I now realized I had heard her cry throughout the whole ceremony. What was this, tears of happiness or tears of sorrow? I really felt guilty. Here again was a lady who never cried, except for when Daddy left, overcome with tears when I married her best friend. I couldn't bear to see her like that, so I talked with Mrs. Fonteneau.

Adrian walked over and put his arms around her. "Feen, stop crying, everything's going to be all right. Charlotte's fine. I promise you, I'm going to take care of her."

I turned back to her and asked, "Mom, are you all right?"

She used her handkerchief to dab at the tears on her face and then her eyes traveled from one of us to the other. She seemed to be comforted by our concern and said, "I'm all right. Dun' min' me. Dunno why I'm cryin'. Well, it done. Y'all married, now."

I eyed the pastor and Adrian's parents and wondered what were their thoughts? They all smiled and congratulated us, evidently accustomed to mothers crying at weddings.

∞

My mother had baked a cake and cooked dinner for the wedding party. Adrian, his mom and dad came over to our house to eat. Mom, Mr. and Mrs. Fonteneau sat at the table in the kitchen and Adrian, Angie and I sat in the living room and ate on our laps. The atmosphere was lighthearted, with jokes being bantered back and forth between the two rooms. For the time being, the problem was solved. I could have my baby, raise him or her, and keep my job. The only thing missing from today was Daddy.

"We can't go on a honeymoon, because we not gonna do what people do on honeymoons, but we can go out and celebrate. Would you like that?" Adrian asked.

"There's only one decent looking nightclub in town and everyone who goes to nightclubs go there. Young and old. I don't want to run into any of my students' families, so if you want to go early, like seven, before the crowd gets there, we can."

"Okay, one drink and a dance to celebrate my fourth marriage." he said with an attempt at a joke, which fell flat.

The name painted on the side of the nightclub was "The High Life Lounge." The building was built with cinder block that was painted gray, and a chandelier in the shape of a candelabra hung from the ceiling in the middle of the room. A booth was situated at one side of the entrance, where the owner's wife was setting up her kitchen. The weekend crowd loved her spicy pork chop sandwiches. A bar ran the entire width of the back wall. The tables and chairs were made of wood painted black, and they occupied both sides of the long room, leaving a dance floor down the center. A jukebox was nestled in a corner and a blues song was being played very loud. The room was smoky, although only a few early arrivals were there. When the song Adrian had selected came on the jukebox, he rose with a flourish and extended his hand to me. I entered his arms and swayed to the music. It felt divine. I closed my eyes and laid my head on his shoulder and floated to a place where I escaped from these last months. He smelled like Christmas spices. He hummed the song in my ear, and then it was over much too soon.

More people came in and Adrian said, "You're not enjoying yourself, are you? You're worried about kids seeing you here. We can go."

I started to tell him I would love to dance one more time, but decided not to. He had not signed up for romance. "Yeah, I'm ready to go," I lied.

We drove around for awhile and were back at my mom's house about nine o'clock. She and Angie were still up.

The plan was that I would stay at my mother's house until Thursday night. That's when the furniture would be delivered to our rented house.

He kissed me on the cheek and said goodnight to everyone. Adrian would sleep at his parents, because there was no place for him to stay at Mom's house. "Are you coming with me to church tomorrow?" I asked.

His eyes opened wide and said, "I hadn't thought about it. Are you going to church tomorrow?" he asked.

"Yes, I am going to church. Being newlyweds, I would like for you to come with me." I said.

He nodded his head. "I was going to go to Mt. Pleasant, my home church, but I'll go with you, instead. I'll be by about ten forty five and we'll go to church. And then you can come by our house."

"Ok," I said.

When I went back into the house, I asked my mother, "How was it on your wedding night?"

She looked up at me, absolutely startled. "My weddin' night. Hmm. Girl, dat was a long time ago…" She looked up in the air to her right as if she were trying to remember. "My weddin' night," she repeated. Then she said thoughtfully, "Ah's still grievin' fur my ma. She'd jes died." Then she smiled, "But, it was fun. It was scary, yet I felt safe at de same time. Ya daddy was so sweet, kind and gentle." She sat silent for a second with a faraway look in her eyes. Then she seemed like she had awakened from a dream and looked at me saying, "Why ya axing me 'bout that? Ya goin' home wit' Adrian tonight?"

"No, our deal is still on. I'll move in Thursday when all the furniture is there. Well, today being my wedding day, I just missed Daddy today, that's all."

"Oh yeah, I know what ya mean," she said. "Ah miss 'im too, still aft'r all these years." We both stood in a shared warm silence. It was as though Daddy was standing there in the room to give us comfort.

Finally, I asked, "Mom, over the years, have you ever figured out why Daddy left?"

She sat at the kitchen table and looked up at me. "No, Bay, I have no idea why ya daddy lef'." She paused, "I know ya miss 'im on dis day, ya weddin' day. But, I can't he'p ya wit' dat one. I wen' from worried to skeered to angry to grief. Den I put it in God's han'. If I coulda, I woulda got him yer fur ya."

"I know you would have, Mom." I hugged her. It had been a

long day.

I spent my wedding night in my childhood bedroom with my sister, Angie.

The next day was Sunday and it was a warm, sunny day. A good day to face the gossip mongers of my church.

My mother and Angie accompanied us to church. Faces turned to study Adrian and me as we entered the sanctuary. They tried to see if they could spot some form of deception or telltale sign of sin. Some of them leaned over right then to whisper to their neighbor. I walked straight ahead with my chin in the air. Mom sat with Keykey's widower and daughter and the rest of us sat in our usual pew midway the church. The usher came over and gave us fans. Because by the time church was over, it would have warmed up quite a bit outside, and I was already a little warm from the piercing stares. I could have chosen not to come today, but I felt it better to confront this head on.

As the choir sang, I wondered if Adrian and I had passed the test of the church members. I knew they were trying to figure out if we were really in love or if this was some kind of trick. Adrian put his arm on the pew behind me and encircled my shoulder and pulled me close to his side. I didn't resist. In fact, I leaned further into him.

He whispered in my ear, "Are you okay?" It felt so good to feel the protection of his body.

I said, "Yes, I'm fine."

"Well, how am I doing?" he continued.

I smiled and laid my hand on his knee, "Great. You are doing great." Right now, you are everything I need, I thought.

When the pastor started his sermon, he said, "I officiated at a marriage ceremony yesterday, Brother Adrian Fonteneau and Sister Charlotte. When I was deciding what I was going to preach today, I thought about marriage and what is involved in having a good marriage. My text today comes from Genesis second chapter, twenty fourth verse: Therefore shall a man leave his father and his mother, and shall cleave unto his wife: and they shall be one flesh."

As he continued his sermon, he talked about marriage and the duties of a man and woman within the confines of marriage. As I listened to the rise and fall of his voice, which at times became a song that seared the heart, I wondered what emotions would be flowing through me if this were a real marriage. Would I be questioning my decision more? Would I be expecting more of Adrian? Suppose I had married Ray, would I still be aglow from our wedding night, instead of having slept in my childhood bed? One thing I knew for sure that I felt was relief. I did not feel indecisive about this marriage at all. I would not have to bow my head in shame before my church members and my co-workers at school and I felt immensely grateful to Adrian.

At the end of the service, we stood on the church grounds, and received congratulations and well wishes from the congregation. No one asked any questions that would have been difficult to answer. It seemed as though everyone was taking our marriage on face value.

∞

When I came out of the principal's office on Monday, I bumped into Ray. He said, "Excuse me, and by the way, congratulations."

"Thank you," I said. Exiting the situation was my desire at this point.

"I heard you all went out Saturday night," he asked as he turned to walk with me.

"Yes, we did, why?" I answered and tightened my jaw.

"Well, it just seemed funny to me, you all would go out on your first night of marriage. Most people are on their honeymoon, or if not, they're at home getting it on. They can't keep their hands off of each other. However, you all were out on the town," he said. "It just doesn't make sense to me."

"What we did on our wedding night is not your concern," I answered. My body tensed and my pulse raced.

"I just want you to realize this marriage is a farce and you need to rethink what you're doing. It's not too late," he said.

"Yes, it is too late" I said. "I am married." I walked into my room and closed the door not to create a scene. He seemed to have gotten the message and walked away.

CHAPTER 12

We heard the sound of music, people's laughter and children playing before we reached Adrian's parent's home. The gray unpainted house stood about four feet off of the ground, with a gabled tin roof and a huge yard with azaleas. Today the yard was bustling with people. In my mind's eye, I saw Adrian's nieces, nephews and myself as we played patty cake underneath that house when we were children. Cars and trucks lined the road and a truck sat in the large back yard.

Adrian told me soon after our marriage that his parents would give us a Bouchérie to celebrate our wedding. I was very flattered they wanted to do that for us. So, today we arrived at ten o'clock a.m. The Bouchérie had started about seven a.m.

A Bouchérie (Butcher) is a celebration in the Creole tradition where neighbors and families come together to have a feast that featured a roast pig or hog. The men killed a fattened pig, butchered it, fried pig cracklings, etc. Almost every part of the pig was used in some way in some dish. The women made boudin, baked sweet potatoes and other side dishes for the meal.

Some children played jump rope and others played dodge ball

as we arrived. "Hi, Miss Ford, Hi Uncle Adrian," said the children in chorus, as we made our way to the large porch.

Adrian looked at the tall trees whose leaves were different shades of yellow, brown and gold, and said, "October has perfect weather for an outdoor party."

"I agree."

The women were in the dining room and kitchen, where they were talking loudly and preparing the meal. The air was alive with the smell of onions, garlic, shallots and other spices, as well as pork in various stages of being cooked. They all turned to greet us as we entered and offered their congratulations. Adrian spoke to his mom and then took time to speak and kiss the cheeks of all the ladies there, while they all smiled up at him with adoring eyes.

I shook my head and thought to myself that he really knew how to appeal to ladies. Then he went outside and joined the men.

I stepped to a window and watched as he entered the yard. Groups of men dotted the back yard, grouped around long tables in different stages of butchering the pig. He approached each group of men and shook their hands. Their faces glowed with pleasure and patted him on the back. He moved on and chatted with his father and other men who surrounded a huge cast iron pot, the size of a washtub. The liquid in the pot bubbled from the heat as the cracklings fried. One of the men stirred the pot with a long stick. The air was filled with the fragrances that cooking meats with the different kinds of seasoning creates.

My eyes drifted from the pot back to Adrian. I had witnessed him socialize many times over the years, but somehow this time was different. The feelings that stirred within me were different. I seemed to get lightheaded and it was difficult to catch my breath. He turned and saw me as I watched him. He raised his eyebrows and tilted his head as if to ask me if I needed something. He had no idea that I was simply admiring his poise and his physique. I shook my head to let him know I did not want anything, smiled and turned back to the ladies. My mother had watched me, watch him.

She was not the only one either. One of the ladies, named Sara said, "Well, Charlotte, see you 'miring ya fine looking man, outside." She laughed at my shocked expression. All the other ladies laughed also. "Congratulations. Glad ya hooked him."

A nervous twitter played about my lips and I looked at my shoes. I did not want her to see how uncomfortable she made me. "I was just checking on the progress of the cracklins, that's all."

"Yeah, right," said Sara and then she chuckled again.

A friend of my mother's named Teresa said, "Tried to tell ya mom lon' time ago. Didn't make sense fur 'er to let a fine man lack dat walk around free. She wouldn't listen to me." She laid the corn aside and looked directly in my eyes. "Glad ya got 'im."

Mom just smiled and Mrs. Fonteneau continued to slice onions, as though she had not heard anything.

Sara said, "I'm gonna ask you what ever'body yer wanna ask ya. So, is he as good in bed as he look?" The volume of the laughter rose and then quieted in anticipation of my answer. Mrs. Fonteneau, whose complexion was light as Adrian's turned a bright red and left the room. She seemed to not want to be around when the ladies talked about her son's sexual prowess.

"Miss Sara," I said in a pleading voice. "Please stop."

"Dat's okay. Don't say nothin'. De way ya lookin' out the winda at 'im. I know it was good las' night and maybe dis mornin' too." She waved her hand downward, turned her back and continued to work.

Again, all the ladies erupted in laughter.

My neck and chest felt hot. I looked down at my feet and said, "He's a good and kind husband." I hoped that would end the questions.

She mimicked me, but in a sexually laden groaning voice, "Oh, ya so good and kind." The women continued to laugh and talk in low tones to each other.

Mom said, "Y'all leave 'er alone, now. She not gonna talk 'bout 'er husband wit' y'all. Leave my chile alone."

"All right, Feen. Jes' having fun s'all. Charlawt, a bit of advice. Dun wear ya self out. It'll be some dar tomarra."

"Yeah, it will. Sho will be some dar tomarra," the other ladies said.

A deep breath escaped my lips. Even though it was all in fun, I was glad my mom had come to my rescue.

When it was time to eat, another long table was set up outside, under two of the pecan trees that dotted the yard. It was covered in white table cloths and laden with cooked pork roast, pork chops, baked potatoes, corn on the cob, boudin, both white and red, and various other Creole dishes. Everyone sat around it and offered their best wishes to Adrian and me. Mr. Fonteneau gave a short toast, simply saying, "Welcome to the family." A feeling of acceptance overcame me as I looked upon his kind face.

Music from the radio in the truck added to the festiveness, and after the meal, someone suggested Adrian and I dance together and so we did. He held me loosely as we danced and I glanced sideways at some of the ladies. Miss Sara and the rest of them, all had smug expressions on their faces, as if we danced naked. Except for Mom and Mrs. Fonteneau, who both seemed thoughtful.

Everyone milled around after the meal and Adrian's Mom went inside the house and came out with a guitar. She handed it to Adrian. "Son, play somethin' fur ya comp'ny."

Miss Sara said, "Please sing somethin' fur us. Love ta hear ya sing."

He hesitated for a moment and said, "Y'all, I'm a little rusty so bear with me."

Everyone clapped and encouraged him, so he nodded his head, put a chair by one of the pecan trees to prop his leg on and started to play. He used to play for us when I was little, but it had been a long time, since I'd heard him sing or play.

He first sung and played a hillbilly song about the fun of eating crawfish and filé gumbo that he'd learned from the radio. Everyone clapped and patted their feet. Then he sung, and played a blues song that expressed the heartache of a man whose woman is cheating on him. The mood became somber as fingers snapped and heads moved up and down to the beat. Then he called me over to stand by him for his last song, which was a song about the heart pounding joy of a man who falls in love for the first time and the object of his affections loves him back. A sweet quietness fell over the guests. His voice was so rich and clear and his fingers so agile and masterful. I looked into his hazel eyes as he sung to me and felt as if I was about to drown. His eyes were on my face and they bathe me with their brilliance. Finally, the song was over and the spell dissipated and then I could breath.

I heard Miss Sara say, "Yep, tole ya. They had a fine time las' night. Dat chile mos' fainted jes' lookin' at 'im.

Again, my neck and face grew hot. I timidly looked around to see who else heard her. She was talking to Miss Teresa. No one else seemed to be paying attention to her.

Adrian walked over to and talked with Mom. I decided to try and look at them objectively. They stood very close to each other, looked directly into each other's eyes, and spoke so softly no one else could hear what they said. I'd seen them speak like this all of my life. Why now did I feel a pang of jealousy?

"Mom," I said.

She turned toward me with an open smile, "Charlawt, whatcha need?"

The uneasiness left my body as I took a deep breath. I was right, I thought. There is nothing going on between them.

"Dun worry 'bout Sara 'n Teresa. They jes having fun with ya."

"I know Mom. I'm all right." But I felt uneasy about the effect being married to Adrian was having on me. I hoped my infatuation would pass once we were divorced.

∞

The good thing about a Bouchérie is everyone takes stuff home. Boudin, cracklins, raw meat and a plate dinner. Hence, it was in honor of us, but everyone got a present.

When we arrived home, Adrian looked at me thoughtfully.

"You know, I wondered how we would look together as husband and wife, because of our age difference, but I think we look good together. What do you think?" he asked.

"I think we make a good looking couple." I felt a little flustered as I remembered the banter of the ladies.

I asked, "Adrian, why did you stop calling me Chocolate Princess?"

His head turned quickly toward me and his eyes opened wide. He sat on the sofa and I followed. "Do you remember the first time I called you that?"

I nodded, "Yes. We were at Aunt Rae's house and all the little girls had gotten colored dolls for Christmas and I started to cry because everyone else's doll was light skinned or medium brown skinned like they were, mine was not dark skinned like me. You took my doll, left and when you came back, she was the same color as me. When you gave her to me, you said 'here's your chocolate princess and she's almost as pretty as you are'."

"Wow, you remember all that. I took her home and my mother mixed up some food coloring and dyed her darker," he said.

"From then on you called me Chocolate Princess and then you stopped. When you called me that it made me feel like I was special to you, even more special than Mom."

"You were and still are special to me," he said as he took my hands into his. "Calling you Chocolate Princess or just Princess by itself, was fine when you were a little girl, or even a very young teenager. Once you began to blossom into a young lady, I didn't think I should call you that. It didn't seem right. It would make me seem like a dirty old man. And I never wanted to be a dirty old man. Feen always trusted me around y'all girls, and I never wanted to betray that trust or even give anyone a hint that my motives were not on the up and up."

"Aww," I said as realization set it. "Wow, so you were being respectful, and I was feeling betrayed and deserted. Like 'why am I not his princess anymore?' "

He took a deep breath, "Char, calling you Princess now would mean a very different thing than calling you Princess when you were a child." He opened and closed his mouth. He seemed to be searching for the right words. "It would mean a certain kind of relationship."

"I understand what you're saying. It's okay. I'm glad I asked because I have always wondered. By the way, you sounded wonderful today."

"Why, thank you, Charlotte. I hadn't done that in a long time. I enjoyed it. I'll have to set aside some practice time and do that more."

At that remark, I thought to myself, please don't do it when I'm around. Because, like Miss Sara said, I'll probably faint.

∞

I saw that my clothes no longer fit, and I began to wear larger sized clothes. Ray had not tried to talk to me in private since he'd congratulated me right after my marriage . However, he watched me closely whenever he was in my vicinity and by December, it was evident I had gained weight and that I might be pregnant.

He entered my classroom at the end of the school day. I knew what he would ask me and I did not know what I would tell him.

"Charlotte, are you pregnant?"

"What makes you think that?" I answered, with my brows drawn together.

"Is that why you got married? Does he think it's his child?" he asked. I did not answer.

He said, "Answer me, please?" He repeated, "Answer me, Charlotte."

"Does it matter?" I asked, in an agitated tone. "Really, Ray. Does it really matter? I am married, which means you are off the hook."

He took a deep breath and said, "So, it is true. You are pregnant. That's why you rushed into marrying this guy."

"His name is Adrian."

"What did you say?" he asked.

"His name is Adrian. You always refer to him as this guy. This guy was kind enough to do me this favor and he deserves to be talked about with respect."

"So, he does know this is not his baby. Why is he doing this? Did he have a crush on you already and is taking advantage of the situation?"

"Look Ray, please. I have to go."

"I know. You have to pick up your mother. You always have to pick up your mother," he added frustrated. "We need to talk."

"About what?" I asked. I was fed up with questions and his self-righteous attitude. "Yes, I am pregnant. Yes, I am married, so it's handled. Yes, you are married. So, I protected both of our jobs and your marriage. I will raise this baby. Don't fret yourself about it. Now, I have to go."

"I love you, Charlotte," he pleaded as if he suddenly realized he might lose the argument.

"You love me?" I asked. "Really? I have to go. Don't you

know the hollow ring those words have? Action speaks louder than words. I have to go."

"Okay," he said. He shook his head as if to say no. But he walked away slowly, deep in thought. He had little choice but to accept what I said, because in order for him to be able to make a fuss, he would have to tell his wife what he'd done. He did not want to do that. Therefore, he would have to accept my decisions on the matter.

I still felt that rush in my stomach when I was around him. I don't know if I will ever get over him. I still felt hot around my neck whenever I think about our night together. The only good thing about it was I knew that my baby was conceived in love.

Because I thought about our night together, it made me feel disloyal to Adrian. Then, I reminded myself that Adrian was a temporary situation. No matter how nice he was, he was only doing me a favor. Why would a well-traveled man like Adrian want a naïve girl like me? Because that's the way he thought of me. Therefore, I vowed to keep my feelings in check and to concentrate on what I needed to do to have a healthy baby and to develop the skills I will need to raise it alone. The two men who were presently in my life were not options. Ray, because he was married and Adrian, because we were not in love with each other.

CHAPTER 13

The bus station was dark, with a small beam of light that came in through one window. The floor looked wet and was caked with dirt and the smell of urine and rancid liquor was so strong that it was difficult to breath. At least the side of the station with the sign that said "Colored Only" was like that. The other side with the sign above the door that said "White Only" was in a separate room. A foreign land I was forbidden to enter or see. On the "Colored" side, there were two drunks who'd sought refuge from the cold. They'd probably gotten drunk at the corner bar and now slept on the only two benches available for seating. After not finding a clean place to sit and being looked up and down by another vagrant, I decided to wait outside. It was cold, but safer and I could breath.

I waited for Eric, Adrian's son from Houston, in my car. Adrian had not seen him since we had gotten married. So, we invited him to come visit for Christmas.

A slim young man with the same posture and build as Adrian's just, not as tall, got off the bus with a bag and looked around. "Hey Eric," I said.

His head followed my voice and his eyes found me. I smiled as he walked over.

"I guess you must be Daddy's new wife," he said. His tone was terse and I wasn't sure whether he was being sarcastic, so I decided to believe that he was not being sarcastic.

"Yes I am. Glad to have you."

"Why Daddy didn't pick me up?"

"He's working and it's Christmas break and I'm off. I thought it would give us a chance to get to talk."

"Oh. Okay," he replied. "Talk about what?"

By now we were in the car on the way home. "Nothing in particular, just getting to know each other, that's all. Let's see, you're seventeen and a senior this year."

"Yeah, that's right. So, you mean he couldn't take a few hours off to come get me?"

"No, that's not what I mean. He could have, but why should he, when I'm off. That's what married folks do. They help each other."

Eric sat quietly for a minute and then said, "He said something about me staying at Grandmaw's instead of with y'all. Why's that? He said he wanted to spend time with me and he don't even come pick me up. Then he want to shove me off on Grandmaw." He sounded disgusted.

"He is going to spend time with you. Our extra room does not have any furniture in it, so we decided you could spend your nights over at your grandparents and then come over every day and spend time with us. That gives them private time with you too. Everybody wants to spend time with you, including them. Your daddy has activities planned for you all to do. He meant what he told you."

In addition to the reasons I'd told him, we did not want him to spend the night with us because then he would see that we didn't sleep together. We did not want to explain our situation to a seventeen year old.

"I see that you're pregnant. Is that why y'all got married? That's the same reason he and my mother got married. Like my mother say, guess he just don't learn how not to get a woman pregnant." The look on his face was repulsive. My mind raced and I wondered how to reach this young man and not slap his face. I was steadily loosing my patience with him.

"Well, why we got married is not your business," I said in an even toned voice. "What is your business is that we are anxious to have you. Adrian is getting off early today. You will be able to ask him whatever questions you want before you go to your grandparents' tonight."

"Look, sorry if I made you mad. I hardly get to see him, since he's not in Houston anymore. It just really ticked me off he's not here to even meet me."

I was surprised at the hardness of Eric. I saw that Adrian had a lot of work to do in the next few days to reach him. He looked like Adrian, but his eyes were hard and bitter.

"Do you even know who I am?"

Wow, what a strange question, I wondered. I said, "Yes, I know who you are. Why would you ask me that?"

"I've been told you don't like me and you don't want me around. That's why he never calls me or why I wasn't invited to your wedding."

"None of that is true. The reason you were not at our wedding had nothing to do with me or my not wanting you to be close to your daddy. We did decide to get married quickly, not because I was pregnant with your father's baby, but for other reasons I'm not going to discuss. The fact you live in Houston and in school was probably the main reason. Let me assure you, you are always welcome here. I have no reason to not like you. I don't know you. But, I want to get to know you."

The weather warmed up during the day and we sat on the

porch until Adrian arrived home. Eric's face lit up when he saw his father. He jumped off the porch and ran to meet him. They embraced.

"Good to see you, Boy," said Adrian.

"Good to see you too, Daddy."

I noticed a different demeanor all together on Eric when he was with Adrian than he had been with me. He looked like a child who yearned for the approval of his father, instead of the rebellious teen I had encountered.

Adrian nodded toward me, "How do you like my wife?"

"She's real pretty, Daddy," he answered.

Adrian slapped him on the back, laughed, winked at me and said, "She sure is."

My heart melted. I wanted to run out in the yard and hug him, but I understood what our deal was and I intended to honor it.

∞

On Christmas morning, Adrian picked Eric up and cooked breakfast before I got up. When I entered the kitchen, I saw both of them as they sat at the dinette set and ate their breakfast.

I said, "Good morning, you two."

"Good morning, Sleepyhead," Adrian answered. "Your breakfast is on the stove."

"Thank you, Husband. One thing about being pregnant is the sleep is just so deep and good," I answered.

Adrian's raised his eyebrows and his eyes opened wide. I don't usually shower him with endearments and I guess that one took him by surprise. He smiled and nodded after he recovered from the initial shock.

I walked over, fixed my plate and sat down to eat. "Have you all opened your gifts yet?" I asked.

"No, we were waiting for you. But since you're up, let's get to it," he added.

Eric opened his and seemed very happy with it. It was a jacket Eric had swooned over when they had shopped for Adrian's mother. "I love you, my son," said Adrian. He looked at his father and gave him a huge, wide grin.

Adrian opened his present from me. He had a fleece-lined cap with flaps to cover his ears, along with gloves and a matching scarf. He looked at me, smiled and said, "Just what I need while I am doing my yard work."

"That's what I thought," I said.

My present was a motorized foot-soaking tub. I smiled. He had been concerned because my feet and legs had swollen. He also had a footstool for me. "After you finish soaking your feet, you can put them up on your footstool."

My heart swelled and I wanted to cry. Instead I said, "What thoughtful gifts. Thank you very much."

He kissed me lightly on the lips. "Merry Christmas, Wife."

I smiled back and understood the sweetness of this man. I wanted to take his face in my hands and kiss it all over, but I didn't. I wondered if I would be able to walk away without being terribly hurt after my baby was born.

CHAPTER 14

Before I knew it, April was upon us. It was difficult to walk, lie down, stand up, sit down, turn over or do almost everything. I was miserable. I was very anxious for the baby to arrive. One day as I stood in my kitchen, a rush of water flowed down my legs and created a puddle on the floor.

As I lay on a hospital bed, and awaited the birth of my child, pains in my stomach came intermittently. A flurry of nurses came in and out to see how far apart the pains were. My eyes roamed the ceiling and I wondered what in the world was I doing there anyway? Sharp pains traveled across my stomach and caused me to groan. As they became more intense and closer together, I bite my lip, squeezed the side of the bed and screamed. I could hear other mothers-to-be as they moaned in other rooms. "Lord have mercy, why am I here? May I never come here again?" After a particularly hurtful wave of pain, the nurse gave me a shot of something and I woke up in a regular hospital room with Adrian and Mom by my bed. And my stomach was flat.

Lucien Fonteneau was here. I named him after my father. We would call him Luke, for short. He was eight pounds, twenty-one inches long and absolutely handsome. The nurses brought him to me to nurse and I could not get over the wonderment of him. This was my baby, born of me, had lived within me for nine months. I examined him from head to toe. Adrian stood by with a big grin on his face. My mom's face was lit up and her smile was constant. On the other hand, Angie's eyes were huge and her face was very solemn. She looked upon Luke as if he were a doll she'd requested for Christmas. She continually wanted to hold his little hand or touch his little arms. I reminded her he was not a doll.

During my three-day hospital stay, Adrian visited during the day and then went home at night. On the second night, about an hour after Adrian left, Ray Dean walked into the room. We stared at each other for a second and then I told him, "He is beautiful. He is in the nursery."

He said, "I know. I know. I saw him. I came as soon as I heard. I was here when your mom and Angie were looking at him through the nursery window. Don't worry. They did not see me. After I was sure they were gone, I approached the window and asked the nurse to give me a good look at him." He nodded his head up and down and said, "We did good, Charlotte. We did real good. Fine looking boy. What's his name?"

"His name is Lucien," I answered.

"Lucien," he said thoughtfully. "Well, at least you didn't name him Adrian, Jr. That would have really completed the farce," he said angrily.

"What in the world do you have to be angry about?" I said heatedly. "You didn't lie up here hurting for eight hours. You didn't pay a dime toward my pre-natal or delivery care. What do you have to be upset about?"

His eyes opened wide, surprised at my bitterness. "I'm sorry, Charlotte. I'm really sorry. It hurts me that I couldn't do all of those things you just mentioned. I wanted to be there with you and for you during your pregnancy and I want to be a part of my son's life."

I really did not know what to say. Finally, I asked, "Be a part of his life? How? You want me to tell him you are his father. I was an unwed mother. You were already married when he was conceived?" I asked. "Is that what you want me to tell him. How am I supposed to do that, Ray?"

"I don't know, Charlotte. But I don't know how I am going to sit back and not be a part of my son's life. I loved you when he was conceived and I love you now."

"Love is a verb as well as a noun. Love is action, not just sentiment. What we did was wrong and I don't want to hurt your kids or your wife. I don't want to hurt Adrian and most of all, I don't want to hurt Luke. I have to think about what's best for him. At some point, maybe, he should know who his biological father is. I don't know. But right now, I think the less upheaval around him, the better he will thrive. My whole mission is Luke. Please don't just think about yourself and your needs, think about what is best for Luke."

"Charlotte, I don't know what I'm going to do. I may have to tell my wife about Luke. If it means I have to do that in order for me to be a part of his life. I already have one daughter that I can't see. I don't know if I can do that again. You don't love Adrian. Are you seriously telling me that you are going to stay with that man?"

"I am not going to talk about this with you. You haven't earned the right to ask me questions like that about my life. I am glad you saw Luke. But, I need for you to think about what is best for him. I'll be back in school in August. Maybe, we can talk about it then. Right now, I need to heal and get through these first months of his life. All of the books say a new baby is very demanding. I don't need any stress."

"You win," he said. "For the time being, you win. I do need to spend some time thinking on this, because this is very important to everyone. I'll be talking to you. Maybe before school starts, but I'll see. See you soon." He took my hand, held it in his for a moment, then turned and walked out.

I didn't know how I felt about his visit. This is not something I had planned on. I had not believed he would take any interest in Luke. But I should have known, because of the way he loved his other children. Consequently, now I was forced to think about how I would handle things if he made an issue of this.

∞

We took Luke home and placed him in his bassinet beside my bed and Adrian sat on the side of the bed. This was the first time he had even been in my bedroom since the furniture had been delivered and set up. He said, "Well, Char, how are you feeling?"

"I feel okay. I am just having difficulty walking around."

"Don't worry," he said. "I am right here. Your mom brought some food by, so we have a lot to eat and I know how to change and wash diapers."

"Thank you so much. I just can't thank you enough."

"Okay, I will let you get some rest. If you need me to help you get to the bathroom, you call me and I will help you, okay. Don't take any chances on anything. Call me and I'll help you."

He was true to his word. Whenever I called, he came and helped me to the bathroom, deposited me wherever I wanted to go. Then came back and took me back to the bed. He took care of the dirty diapers and prepared my meals. At the end of a week at home, I was feeling pretty good and could assume the duties in the house. I did not go out of the house for two weeks. Then I scheduled Luke's first monthly checkup and my six-weeks checkup. Adrian brought us to both.

CHAPTER 15

She said, "Char, Char, Laura n' de kids are yer." The tremors in her voice sent chills down my spine. Something was wrong for Laura to come home and not let us know that she planned to visit.

I said, "Mom, are you alright?"

She said, "Yeah, I'm all right. Worried, s'all."

"Mom, what are you afraid of?"

"She lef' Rick, cuz he went crazy on 'em. He threaten 'er and de kids wit' a gun. He held a gun on 'em all night and when he fin'lly went ta sleep, they lef' wit' hardly nothin'. She skeered he gonna follow 'er down here." The pinch of my mother's voice rose as she spoke.

I said, "Okay, Mom. We're coming over."

"I hate ta ax ya, Char, but we need he'p figurin' dis out. Need Adrian too."

"Okay, Mom. We'll be there in about thirty minutes."

I told Adrian what was going on and he said he was going over, but I should stay at home with Luke. I told him I was going too. We loaded up Luke, dropped him off at his parent's house and headed for my mother's house.

When Laura saw me, she ran into my arms and cried. I hugged her and tried my best to comfort her. Adrian came in behind me. Laura smiled through her tears and said, "Hi Adrian. Good to see you. Thanks so much for coming. Sorry to mess up your day."

I said, "Laura, what happened?"

She said, "He came home in one of his moods and nothing I could do would coax him out of it. Nothing anyone did or said was correct and finally, he went into our room, went in our closet and got his pistol. When he came back into the living room, he told us not to move or say anything. He never pointed it at anyone. But, he said he was tired of us being ungrateful for the work he did every day to take care of us. We all sat in the living room all night. He sat with the pistol in his hand. He just looked at us and dared anyone to say anything. The kids dozed off and on. But I stayed awake. I was too scared to go to sleep. We stared at each other all night. When the morning light came through the window, he got up from his chair like nothing had happened, went to the closet, put the gun up, went to the bathroom, took a shower and went to bed. I put a few changes of clothes together, and some toiletries, went by the bank, withdrew enough money for gas and food and came down here. Look at my hands, they're trembling. I haven't slept all night and I am afraid to go to sleep now."

"Yeah, I know," I said. I remembered his threats. "He is going to come down here after y'all and this is the first place he is going to look."

I was scared for Laura and the kids, but I was also afraid for my mother. Neither Laura nor I had told her how Rick blamed her for whatever difficulties they experienced in their marriage.

Just about that time, Rick drove up outside. My heart jumped in my throat. Laura's car was parked in front of the house, so I knew he knew she was here. He sat in his car for a moment and Adrian walked outside. I was very afraid for Adrian. Laura's kids' eyes were big as saucers at the sight of their father outside. Laura told them to go hide in my mother's bedroom, since it was the farthermost away from the scene, which wasn't very far, and they went. Except for Lonny, who went in the room, but came back out. My mother put her arms around Laura to comfort and calm her.

"Do you all think we ought to call the sheriff?" I asked.

"Maybe Adrian kin calm 'im down 'n he'll go on back ta Port Arthur," said Mom.

"I think we ought to call the sheriff," I said. My whole body trembled.

Adrian came to the door and said, "Rick says he just wants to speak to Laura for a minute. He feels bad 'bout what he did and he just wants to apologize and then he'll go on back to Port Arthur and give her a chance to cool down."

Laura said, "Well, since you all are here, I guess it will be okay."

Adrian turned and gestured for Rick to come into the house.

With an anxious look on his face, Rick stepped into our living room. His voice was soft as he said, "I am so sorry, Sweetheart. I didn't mean it. I don't know what came over me. But it will never happen again."

Laura said, "Okay."

"So, go on get your stuff so we can go home. Missed work today, but I can go tomorrow."

She shook her head continually but spoke calmly, also in a pleading voice. "I can't do that. I've heard the 'I'm sorrys' before. They don't last."

"Aw Baby. I love you. Don't mean to hurt you. We can go talk to the pastor again." His whole facial expression was one of a child pleading.

Laura closed her eyes and lowered her head. She shook her head signaling no again, then said "Not right now, Rick. Let's give it some time. Let's let everyone step back from what happened last night."

He said now with a feeling of urgency, "Like I said, real sorry. Been workin' the docks nigh on fifteen years. Loading and unloading. Hard work, and this is the thanks I get. Go down to the union hall and they pickin' other workers 'fore me. Ain't been getting the hours I need lately. And got passed ov'r for a supervisor job. Ain't right."

Recognizing that his demeanor was changing, Laura said, very cautiously, "Sorry about that, Rick. Have you talked to your union rep?"

"I really don't want to get into it now. Not here. You kin help me figure somethin' out on the way home," he said very sternly.

Laura shook her head, but in a quiet voice said, "No, I'm not going home. You held a gun on us, Rick."

Exasperated and losing patience with the situation, Rick said, "But, did you not hear what I said? I am sorry and it won't happen again. Come on. Let's go home."

My mother stepped forward and said in a composed voice, "Rick, let everythin' calm down. Come back 'n a month or so."

"A month?" he said, incredulously. Rick's back stiffened and he rolled his eyes at my mother. The expression on his face changed from the frustrated begging expression to his eyes being dimmed and his lips curled into a frown. Then with his teeth clenched together, he said loudly, "I was talking to my wife. You know that she is actually a good wife, as long as she is not around you. She doesn't have any crazy thoughts, like leaving her husband, the father of her children for a day, let alone a month." He spat out the last word "month."

My mother was surprised at the hatred in his voice, and took a step back. Her eyes widen and she said, "Really? I dunno whatcha talkin' 'bout. I ain't ne'er say nothin' ta Laura 'bout ya. Matt'r fac', I always lacked ya."

Laura said, "Mom, it's okay. You don't need to say anymore."

She was trying to get my mother to be quiet, because we both knew my mother doesn't back down.

Rick said, "Yes, really. You fill her head with all kinds of stuff. I wish you would just stay out of my family business. My family," he said pointing to his chest, "would be happy without you." His voice rose, and he pulled his hand out of his jacket pocket. He had a gun in it. Adrian was behind him standing on the front porch steps and could not see the gun.

It happened so fast. My heart wanted to jump out of my chest. My impulse was to run to him and stop him. But I couldn't get there fast enough. It was too late. It was like a dream being played in slow motion. "I'll show you a month. Josephine Ford, you can go straight to hell," he shouted.

Her mouth and eyes opened wide in shock as he fired the gun. My eardrums felt as though they'd exploded and for a moment there was perfect silence. Her arms flew in the air, her head jerked back and she fell backwards. "Oh no," I screamed, "he shot her in the head." Then sound returned and I heard more screams. I felt myself scream over and over again. I couldn't help myself. It was like I couldn't catch my breath and I needed to scream in order to breath. The other screams were Laura's and Angie's.

Adrian sprung through the air from the steps with his arms outstretched and landed on Rick's back. They both fell to the floor with a loud thud that shook the whole house. Even though his head was on the floor, his arm was still waving the gun. Even in my distressed state, I knew that Rick could not be allowed to keep the firearm. I realized that Adrian needed my help or someone else might become a victim. I grabbed a lamp and began to aim for Rick's head. It was difficult, because the two men wrestled on the floor, and their heads were close together. Fearing he might pull the trigger at any time, I took a chance and with all of my might, brought the lamp crashing to his head, narrowly missing Adrian. He screeched loudly, moaned and then cried out, "Aah, damn. I just want my family home. That's all. Don't y'all understand?"

Right then, Lonny ran across the room shouting, "Daddy, stop. Daddy, stop." He stomped on his Daddy's hand hard, causing Rick to scream again and this time the gun fell from his hand allowing Adrian to get it. Blood flowed from his wound and he stopped struggling.

I ran to Mom, where Laura and Angie were kneeling on each side of her and called her name. Through my tears I could see she had not been hit in the head, but in the chest.

"What's wrong with you, Man," Adrian hollered, out of breath, to Rick. "I trusted you, Man. I can't believe you shot Feen."

"Mom," I sobbed. "Open your eyes, please. Say something, please."

Laura took my mother's face in her hands, "Mom, I'm so sorry. I shouldn't have come here. I knew he hated you." She sobbed. The kids came out of the bedroom now and Laura ran to them, trying to get them to go back to the bedroom.

"Y'all don't need to see this," she said. "Please, I'll tell y'all when to come out."

Adrian hollered, "For God's sakes, someone get a towel and hold it against Feen's wound to stop the bleeding." All of this happened in a matter of minutes, but it seemed like an eternity. "Laura, you get the towel. Char, call the ambulance and the sheriff.," he continued. Before Laura could move, Angie, who was sobbing uncontrollably, brought her a towel.

Laura was a nurse, but I could see her thoughts were not clear. She was concerned for her mother, and her children. Besides that the perpetrator of all the turmoil was her husband. Now, she moved into her nurse mode and applied pressure to Mom's wound. Mom still lay there unresponsive.

Neighbors from down the lane and the next lanes over had heard the gunshot and had run over to see what was going on. It's always very quiet in the country, thus something like a gunshot rings loudly for miles around. Most of the men were hunters and knew what a gunshot sounded like. They helped Adrian tie up Rick, who was conscious, but no longer a threat. The whole time his eyes did not leave my mother on the floor. She looked like she was dead, and he said, "I killed her. I wanted to kill her and I killed her."

Lonny had helped a neighbor hold his father before he was tied up. Now, with his face knotted up, and as tears rolled down his check, he said, "Daddy, how could you say something like that? That's Grandmaw you shot."

I could see the anger in Adrian's face. He said to Rick, "Shut the hell up, before I take your gun and shoot you with it."

Rick looked upon his son's tear drenched face and his features relaxed. He lowered his eyes and his head fell on his chest.

All of this seemed like a dream. After I called the sheriff, I looked at Mom and saw that it was indeed not a dream. It was a reality. I glanced over at Rick and anger bubbled up inside of me.

"You stinking coward," I hissed at him. "You shoot a defenseless woman, because you're having trouble at work. Are you kidding me? A woman who has been there for you and your family." The more I talked the angrier I became. "And you're glad you've killed her."

My hand drew back to hit him, but Adrian grabbed it, "He's not worth it. Let the law handle it."

"Adrian's right," I said. "You're not worth it. But she's not dead. She's not going to die." I spat the words at him, but I ended in tears and prayed I was right.

The yard was filled with people from the neighborhood. Some people had heard the shot and others had heard over the telephone. It doesn't take long for word to spread in a country neighborhood. Our phones were eight-party lines, instead of main lines. Anytime anyone called anyone, there was a chance that someone else may have listened in on the conversation. There were seven other houses attached to the same line. Each house had a different ring and the parties know which one of the eight party members the call was for. Therefore, all it took was one phone call in order for there to be a chance that seven other different houses would know what had happened.

I sat on the floor with Laura, Angie and Mom. Even though she was unconscious, I said, "Mom, I know you're not going to die. I believe if you were, I would feel it in my spirit and I don't. What would we do without you? I need you to give me advice on caring for Luke. Luke needs to know his grandmother's love. I need your ear whenever I am down and out. I need to be able to comb your hair and curl it. Laura needs you to help build her family unit again. Angie needs you to raise her with your Christian values."

Finally, the ambulance and sheriff arrived. The paramedics came in and took the towel out of Laura's hands. They took her pulse and I heard them say she was breathing, just barely. They also bandaged up Rick's head wound which was still bleeding, but not profusely. From the porch, I could see them put an oxygen mask on her, before the ambulance drove away.

I called out to Adrian, "We have to follow the ambulance. We can't leave her alone there."

As we were leaving the house, the sheriff arrived. He said, "Hold on, hold on. I need to ask you some questions about what happened here?"

"We have to go. My mother's on her way to the hospital." I looked at Laura who was standing in the living room and staring at the blood on the floor.

She sobbed. I went to her and put my arms around her and she jumped away and screamed. She leaned over and clutched her stomach until she was almost bent in two. I tried to hold her again and this time, she let me.

"It's not your fault," I said, "but someone needs to be at the hospital in case they need permission to do some procedure or operation. The sheriff needs to know what happened here, can you handle that?" I said and turned her to me and looked into her eyes. "You haven't slept since yesterday. The kids need to rest and so do you. Will you stay here for a while and answer the questions? Then get some rest. Then you and the kids can come to the hospital. If there is any reason you all need to come before that time, I will call you."

Laura nodded her head. I knew she was in a daze. I walked over to where the sheriff questioned Adrian and told him, "Sheriff, Laura can answer your questions about what happened. Adrian needs to bring me to the hospital now."

The sheriff said, "I think I got the gist of what happened from Adrian, but I will need to take statements from all of you, including you. But Adrian can go with you now, and I'll talk to you all later."

"Thank you. Thank you so much," I said. I signaled for Angie to come with me too.

∞

When we got to the emergency room, the doctors had begun to work on her. They told us she was in critical condition and they would do all they could, but it didn't look good. She had lost a lot blood and the wound was near her heart. They needed permission to operate.

The operation took hours. Finally, a doctor came out and talked to us. They'd stopped the bleeding. She was still unconscious and the next forty-eight hours would tell us whether she lived or died.

Nighttime had come and gone, but I could not leave until I knew Mom was out of danger.

As I sat in the hospital waiting room, I prayed "Lord, let my mother live. She doesn't deserve to die like this. Not by the hands of a deranged family member. Please, Lord, let her live."

I saw our pastor coming and went to meet him. He said, "How are you holding up, Char?"

I said, "Fine, just worried about Mom. We haven't been able to see her."

"That's probably for the best. She doesn't need any excitement. Her body needs to find its way back and heal."

About the same time, Laura and her children came. She looked rested and much better than she had yesterday. She still looked worried, however.

"How's your mother doing, Char? I just heard about it and I thought I would come to check up on her." I turned and was surprised to see the dark brown handsome face of Blain Richardson, Keykey's widower.

"It's touch and go, Blain. But I think she's going to be all right. Thanks for coming."

"Well, you know I couldn't have made it without her since Keykey past away. She was there for me and my child and I want to be here for her," he said.

I hugged him again. I felt comforted he was here. Keykey would have been here. Then I turned to the pastor and said, "Pastor, would you pray for Mom and pray for us?"

He said, "Sure."

All of us got in circle and held hands.

Pastor began, "Heavenly Father, we come to you today, because we know you are God and all things rest with you. You are the Alpha and the Omega, the beginning and the end. You said all things work for the good of those that love the Lord. Sister Josephine loves you, Father. Put your healing hands upon her body and make her whole again. Heal her like she was brand new. Heavenly Father, embrace her family. Give them grace and courage. Give them the strength they need to survive this difficulty. We know you didn't promise us that we wouldn't have trials and tribulations. We know you will be with us through those trials and tribulations. Heavenly Father, look down on the poor soul who caused all of this heartache and allow him to see the devastation he caused so his mind might heal. Heavenly Father, we ask that you bring Sister Josephine through this crisis, so we may see her warm smile again. These things we ask in Jesus' name. Amen."

Everyone said, "Amen."

Adrian took me by the hand and led me to a seat. He had been a rock as always. He had gone to his mother's and checked on Luke and had gotten food for Angie and me. As I sat in the waiting room, so tired, I laid my head upon his shoulder and went to sleep. When I woke up, my head was on his lap and my feet were up on the sofa.

A doctor came down to the waiting room and told us we could visit Mom. She was awake, but we couldn't stay long and we couldn't engage in conversation. The tiredness left my body and laughter and hugs went around the room.

Adrian and I faced each other with big grins, and he took me in his arms and held me so tight. I released a deep breath. It felt so wonderful. He said, "I could hold you like this for ever."

Then he abruptly let me go. When I looked into his face trying to understand what had just happened, why had he left our warm embrace, he would not meet my eyes.

When we entered her room, there were tubes all over the place. Her eyes were opened and she looked at each one of us, one at a time. I could see tears in her eyes. The nurse told us we had to go. They did not want to upset her.

The doctor said she had come a long way. She was awake and hopefully her body would continue to heal. He was cautiously optimistic, because he had not thought she would have lasted this long. He advised us to go home and get some rest and then come back in the morning. Thankfully, we went home.

We visited Mom every day and slowly she began to gain strength. She was still not out of the woods, though.

One day while I was running errands and Luke was at Mrs. Fonteneau's, I decided to make a quick stop at the hospital before going home. As I approached the room, I heard Adrian's voice. I stopped because I didn't know that he'd planned to visit my mother today. I walked slowly to the room and peered in. Adrian stood by the bed. His back was to me at the door. He held my mother's hand and whispered something I could not hear. My mom's eyes were closed and I was not sure whether she was asleep or not, or even if she had heard what he said. I did not know whether to enter or not. It seemed like such a private scene. After a moment, I decided to walk in.

"Hi there," I said.

Adrian turned to me and laid my mother's hand gently on the bed. He smiled, "Hey Char, I didn't know you were coming this morning."

"What difference would it have made if you would have known?" I asked.

He continued to smile at me in that way that melted my resolve and said, "Well, because we could have come together."

"Yeah, we could have," I said. However, I wasn't sure he wanted me to come with him after the scene I had just witnessed.

"What's going on?" I asked.

"You know how I feel about your mother, Char. We have been close friends for a long time and I just felt like talking to her. That's all. It was a close call. We almost lost her." He paused slightly, "You can't really have a problem with that, can you?"

"No, no, I don't. I was just surprised to see you." I felt silly being jealous, but I guess that's what I was. Now that I was in the room, I could see that Mom slept soundly. She had not heard a word either one of us said.

"Hello. How y'all doing?" said Blain and he entered the room.

"Hi Blain. Surprised to see you again so soon," I said.

"How you doing, Man? Char told me y'all spend a lot of time together?" Adrian said in a questioning tone, gesturing toward Mom.

"She's been helping with Lil Rae and fixes Sunday dinner for us. I mean, I am so grateful to her, Man. Really."

As he spoke, memories of Keykey flooded my mind, and I realized how much I still missed her. It had been almost two years since she'd been gone. She'd always made sure everyone knew how good Blain had been to her, how kind and attentive. He was at least six feet with a slim muscular frame, a square face with soft, kind brown eyes. He wore a starched khaki shirt and pants. He'd worked construction all of his life. I wondered why he wasn't at work, because it was a sunny day. Had he taken off today to come see Mom?

Adrian and I both eyed him intently. Blain shifted his weight from side to side and said, "She's sleeping so I'll let her sleep. I'll come back later."

"Oh, okay then. If she wakes up while I'm here, is there anything you want us to tell her?"

"No, I'll come back later."

"I'll tell her you came by," I said.

"Sure thing," he said and walked out of the room.

"What do you think that's about?" I asked Adrian.

"He just came to see her, that's all. No more. No less. He told you that he was grateful to her. She always sits with him in church. Looks like they have become real good friends. Don't make more out of it than it is," he answered.

"I know you're right," I said

She didn't wake up while we were there, so we didn't get a chance to tell her.

Mom progressed very well and was well enough to come home in two weeks. Laura and her kids stayed at Mom's and cooked and cared for her. Dr. Frank made house calls to his favorite housekeeper and by June, she was able to go back to work on light duty. It was so good to see her up and about again.

Rick made an agreement with the DA's office to plead guilty to second-degree attempted murder. He received a five to ten-year prison sentence. At his sentencing hearing, he read a statement to the family that in effect said he was sorry for his actions, but still blamed Mom for his predicament. Laura planned to divorced him as soon as she's financially able.

CHAPTER 16

It was just amazing how well Adrian and I got along. He always seemed to make decisions about himself and how he was going to handle a particular situation with Luke and me in mind. One day as we drove to a grocery store with Luke, who was about three months, I asked him, "Why didn't you and any of your wives stay together? You and I get along fine. It seems like you are a perfect husband."

He laughed. "That's because I am a pretend husband. I might not be such a good husband, if we did everything that married folks do."

"What do you mean? We have come through a lot of situations married people go through, including renting a house, buying furniture, meeting and dealing with in-laws, stepchildren, finances, family tragedy, you name it. The only thing we don't do is make love. I can't see how that one thing could make that big a difference."

"You are correct. That is the only thing, but it is a biggie. We don't have the tension and jealousy that happens when a husband and wife have a good time together in the bedroom." Talking about making love took my mind where I didn't want it to go.

"I see what you're saying," I said. "But, you never talk about your other marriages. Why?"

"I really didn't want to get into it, but I will hit a few highlights for you" he said. "My first marriage, which was Eric's mother, happened when I was twenty years old, stationed at Ft. Hood Army Base in Killen, Texas. She was young and pretty and exciting. I was a l'il ole country boy and neither one of us had any idea what marriage was 'bout and what it involved. Anyway, we got married, cause she was pregnant. When I went on assignment to different places, she stayed home and it's hard to keep a marriage going like that. She met someone else and so did I and we divorced. My second wife, I met when I was overseas, in Germany. She was a white German girl, and I don't know what I was thinking. Because I knew I couldn't bring her back to the states with me, visit my parents in the South and remain alive. But I didn't have to worry about that because we ended up not being able to get along. She had a bad temper and we would have awful, scary fights. I knew I would hurt her one day, so it was best if we parted company. My third wife, I met in Houston. My first wife moved to Houston with her new husband and on one of my trips to see Eric, I met this amazing, beautiful lady. She was strong-minded and self-reliant and we were happy together. She died five years ago in a car accident."

I gasped, "I didn't know that. You never told me that. Strong-mind and self-reliant, huh?"

"Yes, she was. Just like you."

"Wow, are you serious?"

"Yes, I am."

"Well, thank you for the compliment. My mother never told me you had a wife that died."

"Your mother doesn't know that. No one here, except my parents, knows that. I never brought her here to visit. My parents visited us when we lived in Florida. Your mother thinks all of my marriages ended because I was fooling around. Actually, only one of my marriages ended that way. That was my first marriage. I never took the time to explain to anyone. What would have been the point?"

"Well, when you were telling my mom stories about your travels, did she not ask about your wife? Because she does now." I still wondered how my mom did not know about the death of Adrian's wife.

"Yes, she did. I did not come home for two years after my wife died and when Feen asked me, 'how was my wife' or 'do I still have a wife,' I simply said no. I was no longer married. She took it to mean I had gotten another divorce."

"Wow. I never knew that. Why didn't you and your wife visit Louisiana?"

"No reason I can think of. We were just living life and no reason came up for us to come home, I guess."

"Do you have a picture of her?"

"Yes," he said. He reached in his pocket and pulled out his wallet and gave it to me. I opened his wallet to the picture section and there was a picture of Eric, a picture of his parents and a picture of a beautiful lady with dark long hair and eyes, with a medium brown complexion. For a moment, I felt hurt. There was not a picture of me in his wallet. Then I remembered, we were pretend husband and wife, in our minds. Because according to the laws of Louisiana, we were married. I looked at her and felt envious of her. Adrian had loved her very much and evidently, still did.

By this time, we'd reached the grocery store. We entered and Adrian pushed the cart, while I carried Luke.

We were in the produce section, when I noticed Ray and his wife, grocery shopping. Adrian saw him about the same time I did and said, "Well, well, well, speaking of passion filled events, there go your Man," he said sarcastically. I was surprised by his tone. Adrian never spoke that way to me. Then more softly, "Have you ever told him about Luke?" he asked.

"Yes, I did. After we got married and I gained weight, he suspected, so I told him. But I told him he could not be a part of Luke's life," I said.

Ray must have sensed something, because he looked directly, at us and his eyes immediately went to Luke. He tried hard to get a good look at him without being obvious.

"Hi there. Don't you teach school where my wife teaches," Adrian asked loudly and walked toward Ray.

Ray's face had a panicked look. It seemed as though he wanted to run, but then grasped that Adrian's actions gave him the opportunity to see Luke close up. Seraphine Dean turned, looked at us and smiled. I nodded at her and then at Ray. Ray answered, "Yes, I teach at Bethune High School. Same school with Mrs. Fonteneau."

Ray said, "What a beautiful baby, Mrs. Fonteneau. How old is he now?" He continued to look at Luke's face as though he wanted to memorize it.

I said, "Three months."

Seraphine Dean said, "He is big for his age and such beautiful eyes. We have five, you know. Children are such a joy."

I said, "Yes, they are such a joy." Then, I looked at Adrian and said, "Well, we don't have a lot of time, so we'll go on shopping, but it was nice to see both of you."

We went our separate ways, and I hurriedly finished my list. Luke had been quiet, but now he grew restless. We quickly paid for our groceries and I fed Luke with a bottle, once we were in Adrian's car.

I'd noticed a resemblance to Ray around the eyes and forehead of Luke. I didn't know how I felt about seeing Ray. This made it more real to me that he was committed to someone else. I knew he was concerned about Luke. I just didn't know how he would be able to have access to him without details of the affair being exposed.

I asked Adrian, "Why did you speak to Ray? Was it so he could see Luke?"

"Well, I have another son, besides Luke, and I know how it feels not to see him. Not to be a part of his everyday life. I thought I would give him a chance to see his son. That does not mean I want him to be a part of our daily lives or of our son's life."

I nodded and I liked the way Adrian said "our son," because that's exactly the way I thought of him.

"Well, Char, how did it feel seeing him? Does it make you want to reconcile with him?"

"Reconcile? Reconcile means that we were once together. We were never together," I said. "No, I do not want to reconcile with him."

"So, did your heart go thumpity thump when you saw him," he continued to question me.

"No," I said with a frown. "I can't believe you're questioning me about Ray."

"Oh, you can ask me questions about my most intimate feelings and past, but I'm not s'pose to ask you nothing?" he asked incredulously.

I laughed, "Okay, you are right. If I can ask questions, then you can ask questions. To answer your question, no. My heart did not go thumpity thump. Go ahead, ask me something else. Ask me anything you want."

"Never mind. I'm fine. I'm fine," he said quickly. We drove home in silence, deep in our own thoughts.

CHAPTER 17

Luke lay on a blanket in the middle of my living room, while I prepared dinner in the kitchen. I heard Mom call my name at the front door.

"Hi Mom," I said, "Glad to see you. Come on in."

"How do, Charlawt," said my Mom as she picked up Luke. "Where Adrian?" She inquired.

"He's asleep. Got home late last night from doing yards."

She said, "Ah lack whatcha done ta de place. Ya made yasef' 'n ya fam'ly a nice home."

"Thank you, Mom," I said. "And Luke is sleeping all night now. I am so glad of that."

"Good," she said, "Adrian done good fur Dr. Frank and Miss Frank real pleased wit' 'im. She give his name ta somma 'er friends."

"Oh, that is great, but I don't know how he will be able to do anymore, unless he hires someone to help him. He is working himself to death now. He didn't get home until nine o'clock last night. He has Mondays and Tuesdays off, but he does things around here and at his parent's house on those days," I said.

"Well, hiring somebody might not be a bad idea. He a good bidness man." She paused to decide if she should say something else or not. " 'Member Annette Jordan?"

I said, "No, I don't. Who's Annette Jordan?"

"One a' Adrian's ole girlfriends," she said. "She was crazy 'bout 'im when theys in hi' school. Fact, I think dat they wuz crazy 'bout each other."

"If she is Adrian's age, how do you know what happened to them in high school?" I asked.

"Ever'body knew. I tell ya, theys de talk 'a de town. De couple."

"Oh my. Well, high school was a long time ago. She's probably married with children," I laughed.

"No, she ain't," said Mom. "Fact, she always say Adrian de one dat got away. He de lov'uh 'er life, 'n if 'n she had ta do it all agin, she would do it diff'rent and dat she would haf Adrian Fonteneau."

"Hmm, so when is she going to be home and do you think that she knows Adrian is back living in Marksville?"

"She comin' fur the Fort 'uh July. There is gonna be a dance de Sad'day night. Gonna be a reunion party, since folk come home fur de Fort."

"Well Mom, Adrian is grown and is his own man. If he is interested in Annette, there is nothing I can do to stop him," I said.

A frown crossed Mom's brow, "Whatcha mean by dat?"

"Mean by what?" I asked.

"Nothin' ya kin do 'bout dat. Dat man ya husband. He not 'vail'ble to 'nother woman," she said.

She surprised me by saying that. "Well, Mom, you know what my arrangement with Adrian is. You know we are just playing married."

"Playin' married? Theys lotsa marr'ages' don't haf de

understandin' y'all haf," she said. " 'Sides, Luke mos' three mont's ole now 'n Ah ain't hear'd nothin' 'bout no divorce." Our eyes locked, because she knew she had made a good point.

"You're right, Mom. When we were talking about getting married, we really didn't set a date for the divorce and neither one of us has brought it up since Luke's been born. To tell you the truth, I am perfectly content with the situation. Luke has a loving father and I have a caring and supportive partner, so I'm fine. However, I don't know if I can continue asking him to put his life on hold for me."

My mother's eyes opened wide, and said "Girl, ya bett'r stop and think 'bout whatcha jes said. Think 'bout whatcha want and don't want. I ain't nev'r seen ya dis happy. Think 'bout if ya ready ta give dat up, 'n if ya not, start thinkin' 'bout how ya kin keep whatcha got."

Adrian, who had been taking a nap in my bedroom, walked into the room. As always, he was glad to see my mother, and they talked to each other like they used to when I was a kid, like I wasn't even there. I excused myself and went into the kitchen and took a load of diapers out of the washer.

When I returned, Mom said, "I'm on my way to the grocery store, I'd jes stopped in ta see y'all. Since Laura and the kids here, haf ta go pretty often. 'side dat Ah wanta fix a dish 'n make a cake fur Blain 'n lil Rae. So's they kin haf somethin' fur Sunday dinn'r 'ready done."

"You spend a lot of time over there, Mom. I know you like to help, but with Laura's kids at home, do you think you have the time? I mean it's been a while now since Keykey passed and maybe Blain needs to be learning how to do some of those things on his own."

"Thought you would be glad I'm he'pin' Keykey fam'ly out," she stopped and studied me closely. "Since when ya worry 'bout where Ah go and who Ah do things fur?" she asked.

"Since you have been spending a lot of time around a man young enough to be your son. He's thirty-four years old, Mom." I emphasized

Her back stiffened and she looked from Adrian to me. "Well sir, ain't dat somethin'. De pot callin' de kettle black. Y'all done furgot y'all not zackly de same age no. Anyhow, ain't nothin' lack dat, Charlawt. If'n it was, ain't ya bidness," she answered.

I looked at Adrian, who had calmly sat and watched the scene, and said, "Talk to her. She won't listened to me. She'll listen to you."

He opened his mouth, then closed back, and then said, "Feen, not judging you or anything like that. Not saying nothing is going on. Just asking if you sure you know whatcha doing? That's all Charlotte's saying."

Her eyes got big and her eyebrows moved up in surprise. "Adrian, can't believe ya tellin' me somethin' lack dis. Nothin' goin' on twix him 'n me. But, if'n there is, maybe Ah need somebody sometime?" She tilted her head to the side and said. "Ya got Charlawt and Luke. I kin see ya happy and I'm happy fur ya. But sometimes Ah need somebody." She stood with her hands on her hips glaring at him.

He stood up and looked down at her. "Of course, you do. You deserve someone. The right someone."

"Ah haf ta worry 'bout 'is age. Y'all don't. Well sir, ain't dat somethin'. Let me tell y'all somethin'. Ah's a grown woman, 'n I kin choose fur myself. Y'all bett'r sweep 'round ya own front door 'fore you come ta sweep 'round mine. Now, Ah gots ta git ta de store." She turned and stormed out of the house.

We walked out on the porch and watched her drive off in Laura's car. I said, "Thanks for trying to talk some sense into her. I don't understand what's gotten into her. I hope she hasn't developed some feelings for Blain. I just don't think that will work. Nevertheless, I'm sorry we upset her."

"I'll talk to her again. In a calm environment. Wasn't the best time with her on her way somewhere and her mind on other things."

Gazing into his hazel eyes, I wondered what was on his mind. "Why whenever my mother comes around, you all make me feel like I am ten years old."

He scowled and said, "What?"

"You heard me. Whenever my mother comes around, you all start talking about God knows what and it's as if I'm not here."

"Hmm. I never noticed that. But if we do that, I'm sorry."

I looked at him thoughtfully. I had asked my mother before I married him, how she felt about him, but I had never asked him, how he felt about her. I guess at the time, his feelings were not my concern, only hers were. Now, I wanted to know about his feelings. "Adrian, remember the night we talked to my mother about getting married and the two of you went outside, so that I couldn't hear what you all were saying?"

"Yes, I remember. Why?"

"What were you all talking about?" I asked.

"Are you serious?"

"Yes."

"Let's see, if I can remember. I told her that her friendship and respect were very important to me. I would only marry you if she gave her blessing. I would never misuse you or treat you badly. Asked her if I had ever lied to her and she said no. Might have said more, but I think I covered the important parts. Char, your Mom and I were friends and confidants. She leaned on me and I got to admit, I leaned on her. I know some things about her nobody knows and she knows things about me. We were never lovers. But we meant a hellavu lot to each other. Feelings like that just don't go away. But we never crossed the line. I know the age thing matters to her. That's why I don't think there's nothing 'tween her and Blain. Getting back to what we talking 'bout, old habits are hard to break. For a long time, that's how it was when Feen and I saw each other. Very good friends, very glad to see each other and wanting to catch up. But since I know it bothers you, I'll do my best to include you, and never make you feel ten years old again. Okay?"

"Okay," I answered, satisfied with his answer.

"Adrian, you were a friend of my father's. What do you think happened between him and my mom to make him leave?"

"What?" Adrian looked at me astonished. "What in the world are you talking about?"

"Well, I have always wondered what happened between them to make him leave like that and not come back?"

"I don't know, Char," he answered. "I don't know if she did anything to make him leave and not come back. If you think she did something that made him leave, why don't you ask her?" He sounded almost angry.

"I didn't mean to upset you. It's just that I love my mom and I don't want to upset her. That's why I'm asking you. However, it's a little disconcerting not knowing why he's gone or if he is dead or alive."

"Know what you mean. Spent a lot of time over the years wondering what happened to him. I know it's gotta be worse for you."

I wanted to broach a subject I had always wondered about, but didn't have the nerve to ask my mother. "Adrian?" I asked.

"Yes."

"Do you think it strange I look so different from the rest of my family?"

He turned and looked into my eyes. "No, most black families have a lot of different skin tones in their families, and most families have different looks. What in the world is bothering you? Such strange questions today."

"You are probably right," I said. I did not feel satisfied with that answer, but I was not ready to push the subject further either.

Luke began to cry and I went inside to take care of his needs. Adrian went outside to take care of his lawn equipment.

After I'd burped Luke on my shoulder, I pulled the curtain back and watched him provide maintenance to his equipment. He had taken off his shirt and knelt down by one of his lawn mowers. I loved to watch him like this when he didn't know. We were both very careful not to meet each other in the house half dressed. As a result, there weren't any awkward moments. Now, as I looked at his tanned lean body and watched his muscles flex underneath his skin, it gave me pleasure that radiated throughout my body. Suddenly he looked toward the window as if he'd felt my eyes on him. My heart jumped and I quickly stepped back.

CHAPTER 18

It was a bright sunny day and I picked Delores up to go shopping for dresses for the Fourth of July Dance. My spirits were high. It was good to have a day without baby duties. It had rained the day before so the air was fresh. I knew before the day was over, it would be blazing hot.

"Delores, thank you so much for going shopping with me. Since Keykey passed away and Luke was born, I haven't had time for clothes shopping," I said.

"Yeah, I know. I miss her, too. I miss her solos on Sunday. Hmm. That girl could really sing," said Delores.

I smiled and nodded my head. In my mind's eye, I could see her with her head lifted up as she looked to the sky and sung. "Me too. But what I miss even more than that was our talks. It seemed like I was the one who had gone out into the world to become independent, but she was the one with the wisdom. You know what I mean?" I said.

"Yeah, I know what you mean. How are her husband and daughter doing?"

"They're fine. Mom still goes by there on a regular basis,

cooking and stuff. I told her she better stop going by there. People are going to start talking." I chuckled as I thought of the absurdity of her and Blain as a couple.

"Is he seeing someone? It's been almost two years now. He would be a nice husband for somebody."

"Yes, he would. For somebody. He loved her so much. Somebody would have some large shoes to fill, coming after Keykey," I said.

I found a good parking place in the parking lot and saw a car that looked like Ray's car. I did not want to run into him. My heart stood still for a moment.

Delores saw my face and said, "Char, what's wrong?"

"Nothing, just glad to be out without Luke," I lied.

When we entered our favorite store, I felt serene as I walked down the aisles and looked at the beautiful clothes, of all shapes, sizes and prices. Delores and I separated and tried to select items to purchase.

Walking around the store, I noticed a white lady that seemed to appear wherever I was. I looked at her to smile, since we seemed to be interested in the same items and she'd quickly averted her eyes. I wondered what was going on with her.

I picked three dresses and this same lady followed me all the way to where a mirror was located. We were allowed to hold the clothes to the contours of our bodies over the clothes we had on in order to ascertain if the item would fit or not. I wasn't allowed to try a dress on because if I didn't buy it, a white person wasn't going to buy a dress a black person had tried on. While I held each dress to me, I saw the same woman as she hovered by. Again, I tried to meet her eyes to speak and she turned away. I decided the red one would fit. I was elated that I had found a suitable dress so early in the day. The lady continued to stand around and that's when it came to me. She had followed me around because she thought I was there to steal. I was dressed in a suit, with stockings and heels and she still thought I was there to steal. Was it because I was black? Did she think I did not have money to pay for it?

When I came to the conclusion I was being followed, I put the perfect dress back on the rack. I felt warm all over and a nervous energy was upon me. I could not move fast enough. I decided to approach her. Then I saw Delores and approached her, instead.

"Delores, some lady is following me. Is someone following you?"

She looked around and said, "No, no one is following me."

"I was having such a good day. I found the perfect dress, but I'm not buying it from here. I'm so upset. This is my favorite store, too," I said as I moved back and forth. I shook my head. I found it hard to believe what had happened.

"Who's following you?" She asked.

I pointed the lady out to her, who now had busied herself at another rack still not far from us.

"You're sure, Charlotte?" she asked.

"Yes, I'm sure. Come on, let's get out of here."

We found another store, nearby and I hoped we would not have the same experience. I'd hated putting that dress back, because it was the style I'd wanted, but I could not in good conscience reward a store that had labeled me as a thief, because of the color of my skin.

We searched for dresses. I picked out three dresses I liked again. One of them was red. I went through the same process to determine if the dress fit.

Looking in the mirror, I came face to face with Seraphine Dean, Ray Dean's wife. My heart jumped into my throat.

So that's who was in the car I saw on the parking lot, I thought.

"Oh hi, Mrs. Dean," I said.

"Fancy running into you again, Mrs. Fonteneau," she said

sarcastically. Her tone surprised me. After all, when I saw her a few days ago with Ray, she was as friendly as she could be. Now, her eyes were hard and mean.

"Yeah, how about that?" I looked around to see where Delores was, and tried to keep my voice calm. I felt a little apprehensive and wondered what was about to happen.

"Looking for your friend?" she asked.

"Yes, how'd you know I was here with a friend?"

"Because I saw you both a few stores back and I followed you. I wanted to see if I would get a chance to talk with you alone," she said, her tone a little bit better than it was at first.

"Okay," I said, still nervous. My heart thumped away and I prayed for it to settle down. I wanted to concentrate on what she had to say.

After a moment of silence, I asked, "Mrs. Dean, what do you want from me?" I did not want to confront her, but I felt like I had no choice.

"I want you to leave my husband alone," she said. My heart stopped. My fears were confirmed. She knew.

"I'm not going with your husband, Mrs. Dean?" Since I was not sure how much she knew, I decided to tread lightly. "This is not the place to talk about this. Could we meet for coffee sometime?"

"I want to talk now and there's no place near here where colored folks can have coffee, you know that," she said sarcastically.

"Well, this is not the place."

"So prim and proper. Worried about your reputation. Well, you should have thought about that before." Her voice was hard and angry.

My mind raced. Where could we go? I needed to get her out of the store, because I didn't want to cause a scene.

"Wait a minute," I told her.

I went and found Delores.

"Delores, I'm going out to the car. I'll be back in a few minutes," I said.

"Want me to come with you?" she asked.

"No, I'll be back. I'll explain later," I said.

When I returned to Mrs. Dean, I said, "Let's go by my car. There is no need for everyone in the store to know what we're talking about."

She opened her mouth, then closed it back, thought for another second, and then said, "Okay, I'll follow you."

When we reached my car, I turned around and faced her. She said, "Well, what do you have to say for yourself?"

"We didn't have an affair. Where did you hear that?" I asked, my mouth dry and my pulse rate accelerated.

"You are a lying hoe," she said, and took a step backward. She moved her arms back and forth, as if she were about to jump out of her skin. I could see how angry she was. "You're lying. Why are you lying? Y'all think I'm a fool," she said. She continued to move around, but her eyes didn't leave my face.

"No, Mrs. Dean, I am not a whore and nobody thinks you're a fool," I said. "Who told you this?"

"Why are you so concerned with who told me? The fact of the matter is I know and when I saw you and your husband in the grocery store with your baby, I knew it was true. That little baby looked just like my children when they were babies."

I took a deep breath. She knew about Luke, too.

"So, what do you have to say for yourself? You knew he was married. You were so hard up that you had to run after a married man?"

"Mrs. Dean, I am sorry for the pain you're in. I didn't run after a married man. Some of the blame lies with your husband. Have you asked him about it?"

"Don't you worry 'bout me and my husband," she shouted. I

looked around to see if anyone in the parking lot had paid attention. There were a few shoppers, but none of them seemed to look in our direction. The sun beat down on us from overhead and I felt perspiration on my body. "Are you still seeing him?" she asked.

"No, I am not. I am married now, as you know," I said. I hoped that would soothe her.

"What y'all going to do about the baby? Does your husband know it's not his baby?" she asked.

"Mrs. Dean, now it's my time to say don't worry about me and my husband. That's not your business. You need to talk with your husband about what happened between us," I said.

"Well, let me make this perfectly clear," she said. "If I ever catch you anywhere around him, you will pay. Do you understand what I mean?" She stepped forward and her eyes glared into mine. "I will see you six feet under before I let the likes of you break up my family."

I stood frozen. I couldn't believe what she had just said. Anger rose with in me. She had threatened my life over Ray. I counted to ten silently.

"That's right," she continued. "If I don't kill you, I'll mess you up so bad. You'll be flying in the air like a bird. When I'm finished with you, you gonna wish you were dead. You're gonna beg somebody to kill you to give you peace," she took a breath and eyed me. "Do you understand what I'm saying to you?" she asked.

"Mrs. Dean, we work together at the same school, so I'm going to be around him." My world spun and I felt faint. I thought about what my mother had said about her being "strange" from Miss Teresa's family of hoodoo root doctors. I knew her threat was about hoodoo and how she would torment me. I prayed to my God to protect me from whatever spells she had in store for me. There seemed to be something wrong with this woman.

"I'm not worried about at school. He's not going to do

nothing there. He's too afraid of my brother. I'm talking about away from school," she said. "How many times did you see him?"

"Mrs. Dean, calm down."

"Don't tell me to calm down. Answer my question."

"I am not getting into that with you. Like I said, talk with your husband and stay away from me," I spoke just as forcefully as she had spoken. "I have a son to raise and I don't need to be threatened by you."

"Sweetheart, that's not a threat, that's a promise. Stay away from him." She spat the words at me as she turned to walk away. Then she turned, walked back to me, pointed her finger and said, "You think you're cute. Well, I'm cute too. But I will hurt you. Believe that." She whirled around and walked to her car.

I saw Delores coming to the car with a shopping bag.

"Was that Ray's wife you were just talking to?" she asked.

"Yes, it was," I said. "I saw them in the grocery store the other day and she just wanted to ask me how Luke is." My heart raced.

"Girl, you're soaking wet. You've been out here in this heat since you left me?"

"Yes, I have." I did not want to explain that it was a combination of heat and stress. "Ready to go?" I asked. Right now, I yearned for the safety and tranquility of my home.

"Sure, where are your bags?" she asked.

I rubbed my chin and said, "Don't have any. Oh well, I'll just wear my wedding dress. It's a party dress. I'm not going back in any store today."

What a day this was? I'd found two perfect red dresses and had not bought either one of them. Besides that, I was wet all the way to my panties. Not the fun day I'd expected to have.

When I walked into the house, Adrian's eyes opened wide. "Back already?"

"Yeah," I answered. I did not want to discuss any more about it. "Were you okay with Luke?"

"Yeah, we got along fine. Charlotte. You know that Luke and I are buddies. Where have you been? Did it rain in Alexandria?"

"No, why?"

"'Cause your hair is plastered to your forehead and your dress looks like you were out in the rain."

I walked into my bedroom and looked at myself in the mirror and prayed. I hoped this was the worst retaliation that I would receive from Mrs. Seraphine Dean.

CHAPTER 19

I tried to put that horrible shopping day behind me and made cinnamon rolls. Adrian loved my homemade rolls and even though I had not gotten back down to my pre-baby weight, I thought I'd treat myself. Then the phone rang.

"Charlawt?" My Aunt Rae asked.

"Yes, it's me, Taunt Rae. How was your checkup in New Orleans?"

"Oh, it went fine. Doctor say don't haf ta go back til three months from now. Ever'thin' good."

"So glad to hear that."

"Charlawt, I got somethin' to tell ya 'n Ah dunno where ta start."

"Taunt Rae, the best way to do that is just to say it."

"Well, Ah was at de hospital 'n Ah seed somebody. Looked lack Ah knowed 'im. Went round my diff'rent doctors fur diff'rent zaminations 'n Ah seed 'im agin. Dis time he seed me and de look on his face, I knew it was him."

What in the world was Aunt Rae talking about? I couldn't make heads or tails of what she'd said?

"Okay, so, who did you see?" I asked.

"Charlawt, he yo Daddy." My mouth flew open and I dropped the phone. My head spun and my legs gave way.

My eyes opened and I felt wetness on my face and neck. Adrian had thrown a glass of water in my face to wake me up. I had passed out. He'd placed the phone back in its cradle.

"What happened, Charlotte?" he asked. "You fainted. Come sit on the sofa." He helped me to the sofa and I sat with my head in my hands. "Charlotte, say something."

I opened my mouth and nothing came out. "Charlotte, you're starting to scare me. Say something. Tell me what happened."

I took deep breaths while I gazed into his eyes and finally I found my voice, "Taunt Rae, Taunt Rae," I repeated.

"What about Rae?"

"She went for her checkup in New Orleans and she says she saw…" I couldn't say it. I tried again. "She say she saw…" I stopped again. I closed my eyes and shook my head to signal that this could not be happening.

"Are you saying Rae called you and said she saw somebody in New Orleans?" he asked with concern on his face.

I nodded my head up and down. I took more deep breaths as I tried to regain my composure.

He said, "Gonna call Rae and see what she's talking 'bout got you so upset."

He gave me a glass of water and I reclined with my eyes closed. I wanted him to call Taunt Rae to make sure I had not heard wrong.

I could hear his side of the conversation and I could tell I had heard correctly.

"Are you sure Rae?"

"No, not going to tell Feen. We gonna check it out first and then decide when to tell her."

"Okay. Glad you're all right and we'll let you know what

happened."

He got off the phone, went into the kitchen and poured himself a drink. He came back into the living room and sat beside me on the sofa. "Want a taste," he offered.

I shook my head, no.

"Well, are you up for a ride to New Orleans tomorrow? I can have somebody take over my yards and Momma can keep Luke. So, whatcha say? Want to go check it out?"

"Do we have a choice?" I said.

We didn't.

∞

We left for New Orleans early the next morning. The traveling I'd done was after I'd finished high school and gone to college. Besides Grambling, Baton Rouge and Port Arthur to see Laura, I'd done very little traveling. When we neared New Orleans and crossed over a long bridge, I told Adrian "According to our map, this is the Lake Pontchartrain Causeway, so I've finally come to New Orleans. Wish it was for a different reason." We rode by a cemetery with graves on top of the ground and I found it fascinating. Adrian had talked about the French Quarter on the way, but we decided not to go. We'd tend to our business and then head back home.

We went directly to the hospital. Taunt Rae told us the time period of her examination was eight to ten, so he was probably on the morning shift. We went inside and asked the clerk if they had an employee named Lucien Ford and they said no. It looked like we weren't going to be able to find him the easy way. We sat in the waiting room of the emergency room. We asked orderlies and other employees in or near the emergency room about Lucien. We described him the way Taunt Rae said he looked now, but no one seemed to know who we were searching for. Finally, we sat in the car and watched as people came to and got off work. We were about to give up when we saw a tall older man, who from his walk might have been him. He was dressed in scrubs and he approached an old model car.

"Lucien," Adrian called out from across the street.

The man, who was bent over to open his door, stood straight up and for a moment did not move. Then his head turned and his eyes focused on Adrian as he approached. They stood transfixed. Then they both smiled.

My daddy nodded his head and laughed as they walked toward each other. They shook hands forcefully, like two old friends glad to see each other.

"Damn you old son-of-a gun. How you doing? Man, it's good to see you," said Adrian.

"Hey Man. Good ta see ya too. I'm fine," said Daddy.

I followed Adrian across the street and stood behind him. Adrian turned toward me. "Luke, this is your daughter, Charlotte."

His mouth flew open. "Charlawt, oh my Gawd, ya beautiful. Just lack ya momma, just taller. Woulda knowed you anywhere."

As I gazed up at this tall light skinned man, he looked much older than I remembered, and his straight hair was now completely white. But I realized I would have known him anywhere also.

He walked up to me, and before I could control myself, I slapped him as hard as I could. He flinched, his face tightened, but he did not move. We stared at each other, then he put his hands on my shoulders and brought me to his chest. With that gesture, I burst into tears. I put my arms around him and buried my head into his chest.

"Daddy, I worried so much about you," I cried.

"Oh Baby, I'm sorry. Real sorry I worried y'all lack dat," he said as he stroked my hair. "Ah figur'd somebody would come lookin', after Ah saw Rae yestiddy. Didn't figur' woulda been dis soon."

Drawing back from his chest, so I could look into his face, I asked the question that had plagued me for almost fourteen years. "Daddy why? Why did you leave us … and didn't come back … or even call us and tell us where you were?"

He took a deep breath and shook his head. "Ya not gonna understan', but I'm gonna tell ya 'bout it. Y'all come on ta de house, so we kin sit 'n talk."

We followed him down crowded city streets to houses that were similar to my mom's house, except these were long. Mom always called houses designed like these, shotgun houses. The houses were the width of one room and each room was right behind each other. All the doors were aligned and you could see from the front door straight to the back. The houses were all very close together. Something my mother did not like. She always said that she liked country living because folk did not live all upon each other. She couldn't live in town in "dem quarters," she'd say.

I pondered in my mind, is this what you left us for?

The house was old with gray unpainted sides and a rusty tin roof and it looked even smaller than Mom's house. The porch was small and when we stepped onto it, it squeaked. A middle-aged lady came to the door. "Hi Luke," she said and eyed us as we stood behind him. We entered a small living room, with a coal oil lamp lit on the fireplace and a candle lit on a table. The room was dark otherwise. The walls were papered with newspaper to keep out the wind, and a beige lumpy sofa that had seen better days and two straight back chairs furnished the living room. We took the seats he offered us on the sofa and he sat in one of the chairs.

The lady looked familiar.

"Y'all hungry," said the lady. "Don't hafe much, butcha welcome ta it."

"No, thank you ma'am," we said.

Daddy coughed. I know he didn't know where to start.

"Just say it, Daddy. Why did you leave?"

"Come yer, Honey," he called her back into the room. "Dis yer's Clarice Lang. She's not my wife 'n de law, but she my wife 'n spirit."

"Clarice Lang," I said. "I knew you were familiar. You're Miss Teresa's sister."

"Yes, I am," she said.

"Oh," I said as my memory returned, "Miss Clarice, you left town the same time Daddy disappeared. Did you all leave together?"

She disappeared through long shiny beads that covered the doorway, and did not answer me. Daddy said, "Well, we lef diff'rent times, but we plan ta meet up. We met up here 'n New Orleans. Been here ever since."

Waves of emotion overcame my body. My head felt light and I felt dizzy. I was glad I had the sofa to support me. Adrian put his arm around me. "Char, you're all right?" he said. I nodded and patted his hand before I returned my gaze to my father, "So, all this time I was worried about you, didn't know if you were dead in a ditch. You had run off with your woman?" I asked.

"Don't say it lack dat, Charlawt. Ah always loved Clarice. Feen was a good woman, just not my choice. Ah married 'er cuz 'er momma ax me to. She was on 'er dying bed. I was courtin' Feen, but hadn't cided ta marry 'er. Her momma was worried 'bout 'Feen. 'Bout how she would git 'long after she died. She ax me ta marry 'er 'n, take care of 'er and Ah tried ta keep my word. But Ah nev'r love 'er, least not lack Ah love Clarice. We had Laura, 'n den eight years later, we had you and den twelve years later, we had Angie. I'd say I'd wait til de baby got big 'nuf so's Ah could leave, then they'd be 'nother baby. And Ah jes got tied of waiting 'n not being with who Ah wanted to be with."

"So, you were having an affair with Clarice all of that time."

'Not all of it, but mos' of it. Don' haf no 'cuse fur dat. Knowed it not right thin' ta do. Had wanted to leave fur so long, jes one day 'cided ta do it. 'Member Mr. Nichols Ah work fur 'n de rice fields, after I finish my sharecropping?"

"Yes, I remember,"

"Well, he gimme a check fur my work 'n Ah cashed it at de store. Well, dat check was no good, so Donay Long at the store wan'ted his money back. Didn't haf it. Already spent it, payin' bills 'n such. Well, Donay told me if'n Ah didn't give 'im his money back, he gonna haf me 'rested. Told 'im wasn't my fault. It was Mr. Nichols' check. He say don' matt'r. He got de check from me 'n I'm goin' ta jail." He stopped and took a deep breath, "Y'all want something to drink?" he said as he got up and went into the kitchen.

"No, we're fine." I answered.

He came back with a cup of coffee and lit up a cigarette. "Want one?" he asked Adrian.

"No, Man, I cut that loose a while back. Was making my throat scratchy. You need to stop too. Not good for you."

"Yeah, I know ya right. Anyway, 'member Clarice's son went ta de pen fur writin' bad check. He spent two years in Angola Penitentiary. I'm not gonna go ta de pen fur two years. So dat night, Ah came home and you," he said as he pointed to Adrian, "wer on leave from de Army 'n sittin' in de livin' room listenin' ta music 'n you, Feen and the girls look so peaceful together. Ah 'cided Ah was gonna leave de nex day. Ah knowed you'd take care of Feen 'n de girls. Know dat was selfish of me."

Adrian said, "What? Yes, that was very selfish. You should have let me in on your plans. Don't you think?"

"Yeah, you right. But ya here wid Charlawt. So, Ah musta guessed right."

"Well, Luke, I did the best I could to be a shoulder for Feen to lean on, but you know I didn't live in Marksville. I was in the service. I wish you'd told me your plans. It would have given me some idea how to handle it. I felt helpless, not knowing what to do. I tried my best to protect her and encourage her." He stopped for a minute, then continued, "One thing I haven't told you is that I'm married to Charlotte. We got married last year."

Luke sat very still and then he said, "Really, ya married to Charlawt, not Feen."

"That's right. I'm married to Charlotte and we have a little boy named Luke, after you."

"Okay. Congratulations, Man," he smiled at Adrian, then at me. "Dat mean I'm a grandpaw."

"Yes, you are. But you were already a grandpaw. Laura has three children."

He broke into a wide grin. "She got three? Good Gawd a'mighty. She had one when I left, Lonny."

"That's right Daddy. Lonny is the oldest."

"Dat's good news." Then he frowned, "How's Feen? You know I nev'r mean ta hurt 'er.

Adrian said, "She's fine. You know she's a strong woman. But what you did tore her up inside for a long time, Man. A long time."

Daddy nodded his head. "She wit' somebody?"

"No, she's not. She works, take care of her house and girls. But she ain't got nobody."

I sat listening to Daddy and Adrian as they talked. It was so surreal to me. This man whom I had idolized had simply decided he'd had enough and just left us. My mind drifted away and as my eyes adjusted to the light. I took in the faded rug and round table on the other side of the room with a lighted candle with a saint on it and a Bible. Above the table was a large picture of Jesus Christ. Beside it was a framed picture of a younger Daddy and Clarice and on the back wall above the fireplace was an identical picture of Huey P. Long that also hung in my mother's living room.

"Charlotte, Charlotte," Adrian said as he shook my arm. "You're all right. I have been asking you if you were ready to go and it didn't seem like you heard me."

Daddy sat forward in his seat with a concerned look. "Yes, we have to get back to Marksville. It's a long ride," I said.

"Ah know ya don't believe me, but Ah sho am glad ta see ya," he said.

"I believe you, Daddy," I said. I didn't know whether I believed him or not. My emotions were all used up and all I wanted to do was curl up in a ball and sleep.

Clarice came from the back with a bundle wrapped in aluminum foil and handed it to me. "Jes some corn bread, but it hot. Cut it up in pieces fur y'all. Y'all kin nibble on dat til ya git home. Know it a long ride 'n nowhere fur colored people ta stop on the road ta eat."

"Thank you so much, Miss Clarice," I said. I took the opportunity to ask a question. "Does Miss Teresa know that you live with Daddy?"

"No, she don't," said Clarice. "Teresa ain't nev'r been up yer. Ah only been back home twice 'n fourteen years. We's hardly ev'r talks or sees each other. She woulda tole Feen if'n she knew. Dat's why Ah nev'r tole 'er."

I nodded my head in agreement. I believed her. I felt Miss Teresa would have told Mom if she'd known where Daddy was.

"Miss Clarice, what reason did you give them for moving to New Orleans?"

"Chile, well Ah tole 'em Ah found a maid's job 'n de paper in New Orleans 'n Ah was coming to git it. Part of it was true. Luke found a job fur me 'n lemme know."

My anger toward Clarice started to dissipate. I saw she was doing the best she knew how to do. The fact it hurt me and my family was not all her fault. It was mostly my Daddy's.

"Daddy, I have to tell Mom, Laura and Angie. I don't know when or how I'll tell them, but when I do, I'm sure they'll want to see you too. Can you handle that?"

"Well, Ah kinda knew someday, it would happen. Ah wanta see 'em. Guess Ah was shame ta come aft'r been gone so lon'. Dat's why Ah nev'r came see y'all. Handle it how ya wan'. I'll be fine, cuz I wanta see 'em. Ah wanta see you agin too," he said. He took me by the shoulders and said, "Look me in my eyes. I wanta see ya agin. Okay? Sorry fur everthing. You believe me?"

I laid my head on his shoulder and said "Yeah, I believe you, Daddy. Bye Daddy."

They waved to us as we started home.

"Whatcha think, Charlotte?" Adrian asked me after a while.

"I don't know what to think," I answered. "I am so glad he's alive but, I'm also very angry with him. I could have jumped on him and beat him to a pulp."

"You did the right thing. What good would that have done?"

"Probably nothing, but it would have made me feel better. Hit him one time for each of the times I saw Mom cry over him. One thing that stopped me is he looks like life has already beaten him up."

"Yeah, he does. Both of them look a lot older than your Mom does. That ought to make her feel better," he said.

"Adrian, I know she's my mother and so maybe I'm biased, but how does he choose Miss Clarice over Mom. There's no comparison," I said.

Adrian smiled, "Well, you are biased and Feen does and always has looked a helluva lot better than Clarice. But that's something you can't question. It's not always 'bout looks. They connect in some way. He spoke his heart to you. Said that he loved her then and love her now."

"Adrian, you know Miss Teresa's family deal in hoodoo, don't you?"

"Yeah, I'd heard that. Not sure I put a whole lotta belief into that. Don't know 'bout no miracles they performed or misfortunes they caused."

"Well, I don't believe in it either, but I didn't tell you what happened to me on my shopping trip." Then I went on to tell him about Ray's wife and her threats.

"So, you say she gonna have you flying like a bird in the air, huh?" Adrian said thoughtfully.

"Yeah, that's what she said. She evidently practices hexing and putting spells on people. I was just wondering if maybe that's not what happened to Daddy? You think it's possible he left because Clarice hoodooed him?"

"Uh uh, Charlotte. Don't think so. I tell you, I just don't believe in it."

"Well, I was little, and maybe there were things that happened I was not aware of. But I tell you. Mom and Daddy were always hugging each other and laughing with each other. I can remember hearing them talk in their room after Laura and I were in bed. If he was unhappy, he was a very good actor. If he didn't want to be there like he said, he hid it well."

"I agree on that. They seemed happy to me, too. But like you said, things go on 'tween a man and a woman no one else knows about. He had no reason to lie. He didn't try to make himself look good. He said Clarice was who he always wanted. Beauty is in the eye of the beholder."

I grimaced. "Did you have to say that?"

"Why you ask that?"

"Because Ray said that one time. I wish I could flush that whole experience out of my life, but I can't. Because out of that involvement came Luke and he is wonderful."

"Well, your Daddy, Luke, appeared to have weathered a storm. But he seemed happy enough. Have you figured out how we gonna tell everyone else?"

"I don't know. I'm going to have to pray on it for a while. Let him sweat, not knowing when someone is going to show up at his door. The way we sweated waiting for him to come home."

"I'm a little hungry. Give me a piece of that cornbread."

"Are you serious? Do you intend to eat that? You don't know what hocus pocus hoodoo stuff is in that cornbread," I said.

"Yes, I do intend to eat it. Sweet as that lady was to cook it for us. Told you, I don't believe in that stuff and even if it was true, she's not gonna hurt us. We ain't done her nothing."

"I realize there's a lot in this universe I don't know and a lot of what I know, I don't understand. So, she did seem sweet, but sometimes people do things for no reason at all. I'm not eating her cornbread or anything else she cooks. Ever." I handed him a piece of cornbread.

Taking a bite, he said, "Umm good. Still hot too. Nothing is quite as good as hot cornbread, except maybe hot cornbread and milk. Sure you don't want none? Because if you don't want none, more for me."

"Well, when you foam at the mouth, your eyes roll back in your head, and all of your hair fall out, I'll know why," I answered, a little annoyed because he did not take this hoodoo threat seriously. I put another piece in his outstretched hand.

He chuckled softly. "Girl, you crazy." Then, piece by piece, he consumed the rest of the cornbread.

When we arrived home, I was so exhausted that I went to sleep as I took my bath. Adrian came to my bedroom door in his pajamas, after I was settled in for the night.

"You've had quite a day, haven't you?"

"Yes, I have. I just don't know if I can take anymore."

"May I come in?"

"Sure," I said too tired to even wonder what was on his mind.

"I haven't forgotten our deal," he said.

"What deal?"

"I'm not going to try to make love to you. I just know what a traumatic experience this has been for you. I've watched you struggle with not knowing and now the knowing is not too good either and I want to help you through it."

"Help me how?"

He sat on the opposite side of the bed and lay with his back propped up against the headboard. "Come here," he said. When I looked at him, perplexed, he said, "Trust me, come here."

I moved over where he was. "Lay your head on my chest." I did and then he folded his arms around me. I started to say something and he said, "Sheeee." I closed my eyes and felt his strength and wisdom. My mind still wrestled with questions about how to tell Mom, Laura and Angie about Daddy, and how to deal with the aftermath. But I knew whatever I decided, Adrian was there to support me.

And with those thoughts in my mind, I went to sleep and slept cradled in his arms all night long.

CHAPTER 20

Well, we haven't had a chance to talk all day and I'm anxious to know how the visit went. You know when Feen saw Lucien," said Adrian. We were on our way to the Fourth of July party.

Although I had looked forward to the party tonight, my day had been very emotion filled. Two days before, Adrian and I'd broken the news to my mother, Laura and Angie about Daddy being alive. Mom, at first, did not believe us. "You know Rae can't see good," she'd said. She had to accept it after I told her we'd gone to New Orleans and seen him with our own eyes. She was surprised, and then hurt when she found out about Clarice. Anger set in after that. At first, she wanted to go to New Orleans with Laura and Angie, and then she didn't want to go. Her final decision was to go to and hear his explanations for herself.

Yesterday, they'd traveled to New Orleans for their fateful meeting and I'd gone by my mother's house today to find out what had happened and to give her any support I could.

"No, we haven't had a chance to talk," I said. "Well, I'm not sure how well she's doing. She's talking real quiet-like and I don't know if this is the quiet before the storm. I asked her what he said and she told me he said he was sorry for hurting her. She said that she didn't see Miss Clarice, because she never came to the front of the house and they stayed for three hours. She told me he'd cried and hugged Laura and Angie."

"It's hard for me to understand her being quiet today. I'm really worried about her," said Adrian.

"Well, she was quiet, and she did cry. I could see she was trying not to, but every now and then, tears would just roll down her face. Adrian, I tell you, it tore me up. He was gone, but at least she had dreams and ideas of what he was and what they'd had and now that's gone too. She told me, 'Charlawt, Ah loved dat man with all my heart 'n soul 'n I thought he loved me too. I wooda bet my life on it. Now he say it all a lie'."

"Did he give her any idea of how he might make it up to her?" Adrian asked.

"She said he told her that he would have sent her money to help take care of us, but he never had any. Angie is still underage, so she will try and get child support from him for her."

"Yeah, she can try. Although I don't think she can get much," said Adrian.

"Well, she is going to try. She is so angry. Like I said, quiet before the storm."

When we arrived at the Fourth of July party, I saw Herb and Delores at a table and Adrian and I joined them. The celebration was in the school auditorium. It was decorated with a round-mirrored ball in the ceiling, confetti and balloons. The band had not started to play yet and the tables were half filled. I knew they would be filled by night's end, because it was a sellout. Marksville was a small town and there weren't a lot of social activities to attend. We sat, talked, and observed people as they arrived. I saw a tall attractive lady walk in with some people that I knew, but I didn't recognize her. I said, "Who is that in black?"

Delores said, "She looks familiar, but I can't place her."

Adrian smiled and said, "That's one of my old high school girlfriends. Her name is Annette Jordan."

That name was familiar to me and that's when I remembered my conversation with my mother. I had not thought of it since.

I said, "So this is the girl that liked you in high school and still likes you now, huh?"

He laughed, "Yeah, she did like me and I sure liked her, but I don't know about now."

"Well, that's what I heard."

Adrian made a face. "I don't know anything about that."

Herb laughed and said, "Good answer, Brother. Those kind of answers keep you out of trouble."

"Oh, he's not in trouble," I said. "I thought maybe you would want to check with her to find out." I don't know why I said that, because I sounded like a jealous wife and I was not a jealous wife.

Adrian looked at me intently for a moment, and then said, "Maybe I will. Before the night's out."

I could see from the corner of my eye that Herb and Delores were uncomfortable with the turn of the conversation. It did not seem lighthearted anymore and they glanced at each other.

The music started up and the lights dimmed and the massive globe in the middle of the dance floor began to turn. It was party time. The band was good and played both fast and slow dance songs. We had brought our own snacks to eat with our drinks.

Adrian asked me to dance and it felt so good to dance in his arms. The first dance that we danced to was slow. Hearing the romantics words of the love song sent my imagination into overdrive. He held me tighter. I closed my eyes and buried my face in his chest. He smelled so good. He'd worn the cologne I'd given him for his birthday. I imagined how it would feel if we were really married. If I had not asked him to marry me, but he had asked me to marry him. I imagined he'd asked me because he was in love with me and not to save me from ridicule and the loss of my job. I was so lost in dreamland that I didn't realize the dance was over.

He whispered, "Do you want to dance to this song?"

Startled I said, "Oh, no. Let's sit and come back on another song. I don't really like this song." I really did want to sit down because I felt dizzy from the dance. I wondered what was wrong with me.

"Okay Sweetheart," he said.

I looked at him to see if he was kidding around or was he seriously flirting with me. I looked in his face and I could not tell.

Delores and Herb returned to their seat too. She said, "I was watching you all on the floor. It sure must feel good to be a newlywed."

"Why do you say that?" I said embarrassed.

"Girl, the way you too were cuddled up. The love is thick. I wish Herb and I were still in that period. I mean, we love each other, but the passion we had when we were first married is not there anymore."

Herb and Adrian took their seats beside us so our conversation on that subject ended.

Annette Jordan passed by our table. Then came back and said, as though she was surprised to see him, "Hi Adrian. It's so good to see you."

He stood up and she leaned forward and kissed him on his cheek. I felt my face grow warm.

He laughed and said, "Hi Annette. I am glad to see you too. How long have you been in town?"

"I came yesterday and staying for a week," she answered.

"This lovely lady here is my wife, Charlotte," he said as he gestured towards me. "And my friends, Herb and Delores Batiste."

Her eyes passed over me quickly and returned to Adrian. "Will your wife mind if we have a dance later?" She continued to look at him trying to hold his gaze.

He laughed. "I'll ask her. If she says yes, I'll be over and if she says no, then I won't be over. Anyway, you do look good and it was nice seeing you."

"Okay, hope to see you in a little while."

She walked away, and Adrian sat down. Herb looked at Adrian with a sheepish grin. Delores patted my hand to comfort me. Evidently, I was visibly shaken. Adrian said, "Would you like to dance?"

It took me awhile to catch my breath and then I said, "Okay."

He swung me around the floor in a fast swing out dance. We smiled at each other as we danced. He pulled me to him and we circled around in a fast two-step and then he released me and spun me around again and then we were back in the swing out pattern. Oh, how I loved to dance and how I loved to dance with Adrian. He led me superbly. The dance was over too soon and we returned to our table. I had completely forgotten about being vexed with him about that Annette woman.

Herb and Adrian left to go get more ice for our drinks. I'd seen Ray enter the dance alone soon after it had begun. Now he came over to our table and spoke to me. "Would you like to dance, Charlotte?" It was a slow dance.

I said, "No."

"Okay. Why not?"

"Because that is a slow dance and I will only dance with my husband on slow dances," I answered.

"What kind of rule is that? I never heard of such a rule before," he retorted.

"It's my rule, I just made it up." I paused and said, "Look, if you want to ask Adrian if he minds if you dance with me when he comes back, and he says yes, then I'll dance with you."

I saw Adrian and Herb coming back, and I could tell by the look on Adrian's face he did not like what he saw. When he reached the table, all three men greeted each other. Herb and Delores have no idea of the tension between Ray, Adrian, and me and why there would be any tension. At least I didn't think so. Consequently, Herb greeted Ray warmly, and even invited him to pull up a chair and join us. Thank God he declined.

The band started up a different song, and it was a swing out dance song.

Ray looked at Adrian and asked, "Hey Man, do you mind if I dance with Charlotte?"

Adrian looked at him and nodded toward me and said, "Ask her. I don't control Char. She can dance with whomever she pleases."

I saw the triumphant look in Ray's eyes when Adrian said that. I could tell he wanted to say, "See, I told you he wouldn't mind."

Since it was a fast dance, I said, "Okay."

As Ray and I started to dance, I noticed Annette walking in our vicinity. Adrian got up and extended his hand to her and they also came onto the dance floor. Ray could not dance as well as Adrian, so we basically stayed in the same place going backward and forward. We didn't talk because we were too far apart to talk. Through the side of my eye, I saw Adrian swinging out with Annette and they seemed to be enjoying themselves. She looked like she was over the moon.

The dance was finally over and Ray returned me to my seat. Adrian returned Annette to hers and then stopped and talked to some guys who stood near the dance floor. He came back to our table about two songs later, and was quiet.

Soon, it was intermission. Delores and I went to the bathroom in another area of the building. On our way back to the dance area, Ray grabbed my arm and pulled me to the side. He looked at Delores and said, "She'll be back in a minute. I just need to ask her something."

Delores was surprised by the whole scene, but agreed. I think she suspected something was wrong and walked slowly back into the dance.

He said, "Charlotte, I love you. If you say the word, I will leave my wife. You know I have kids and I will take care of them, both emotionally and financially. You know you don't love this guy. You know I am the one for you and I can make this happen. Just say the word."

If I had ever been indecisive about whether I wanted Ray or not, that was no longer the case. I looked at him and I knew I did not love him, anymore. No matter what happened between Adrian and me, I did not want a relationship with him. I still was not sure if I would tell Luke whom his father was, but even if I didn't, I would still have to deal with issues concerning Luke that Ray would want to be a part of. Because he was Luke's biological father.

"Ray," I said. "I do not love you. If I once did, I don't anymore. I have moved on and you need to, too. I know we have some issues to settle concerning Luke, but we will meet and discuss those. Adrian is Luke's father, both in law and in life, and he will be included in any decisions you and I make that concern Luke. Ray, where is Seraphine tonight?"

"Charlotte, look, I told you that we hardly ever go out together. I asked her to come tonight and she said she couldn't get a sitter. So, she's not here."

"Well, there's something else that I have been unsure whether I should tell you. Your wife confronted me in a department store parking lot in Alexandria."

The expression in his face changed from sadness to surprise. His eyes widened and he said, "What did you say?"

Then I proceeded to tell him how she'd followed me and threatened me with hoodoo.

He looked away as if trying to make connections in his mind. "That makes sense now. Some little hints she has been dropping.

She didn't mean that," he said.

"Yeah, she did, Ray. She meant every word. Her eyes. You should have seen her eyes."

He stood almost dumbfounded. "I don't know what to say."

"Were you riding down my road in Hickory Hill the day Adrian and I rented our house?"

"No, I don't know where you live or when you rented a house. Why do you ask?"

"Because your car passed by driving very slowly. I thought it was you. But since your wife threatened me, I believe it was her."

He stood with his brow drawn together. He shook his head as if to clear it. "All of this is news to me."

"Take care of it without putting my name in it. This also concerns me with your having access to Luke. I can't put him in any kind of danger. This was not the sweet lady I saw in the grocery store. This was somebody else. Somebody not afraid to kill the competition."

Even before the threats, I didn't want to break up his family. Keeping his family meant that in order for me to be with him, I would have to sacrifice my happiness and be alone on the side. Meanwhile, he would live his life fully and give me crumbs whenever he got a chance to sneak away. Plus, since Seraphine had made her position known, it would have to be done in such a way as to avoid any hint of suspicion. She had made it clear that I was the target. Not Ray.

"I am so surprised. I thought you would want us to have a life together. That's what I am offering you, and don't worry about Seraphine. I'll handle Seraphine," he continued.

"No," I answered. "I do not want that, not only because it is not the right thing to do for your family or mine, but also because I don't love you. I want you to understand that and accept that. I know you usually have ladies begging for your attention. I'm telling you I am okay. I'm good. I'll get through this no matter what happens between Adrian and myself. Now, I have to go. He'll be wondering where I am. Tell me you understand," I paused. "Adrian and I will get together with you concerning Luke. Tell me you understand what I am saying," I repeated.

He said, "Okay, I understand."

As I walked back into the dance hall, I saw Adrian seated at the table with Annette. They were in deep conversation. He looked up as I walked in, but made no attempt to move. He returned his gaze to her and they continued to talk. Her whole body was turned toward him and she leaned forward in her chair. My heart raced.

I continued on to my seat. Herb and Delores stopped talking when I sat down. I wondered why.

The band ended the intermission and music filled the room. Adrian and Annette walked onto the dance floor. It was a slow number and he held her close. I felt my face and ears grow hot and I lowered my eyes unable to watch them dance. Should I leave? Should I walk onto the dance floor and slap him? Should I sit quietly, then go home and ask him to leave the house? All kinds of thoughts went through my head as I watched Adrian dance with this woman. A pain so fierce hit me in my chest and I could hardly breathe.

Delores said, "What's wrong, Char?" she asked excitedly. "Char, what's wrong?" she repeated.

I heard her, but I couldn't answer. I opened my mouth, but I was at a loss for words. Finally, I said, "I need to go to the bathroom."

She said, "Okay, let's go."

As we left our table and headed toward the bathroom, I sensed Adrian's eyes on me, but I couldn't feel anything. My legs moved, but I am not sure how they moved. He had never shown me such disrespect before and I was not ready for it. When we reached the bathroom, I put some cold water on my face and then went into one of the stalls, put the seat down and sat. I took deep breaths and slowly I felt myself come back to life and suspected that Delores was probably worried to death.

When I came out of the stall and saw her face, I knew I had been right. "Are you feeling better?" she asked.

I nodded and smiled. "I'm okay. I'm not sure what happened," I lied. "That has never happened to me before." She gave me a glass of water and I drank it. "I guess coming out after having been at home so long did not do me well."

She looked at me as if to say, cut the crap. What she actually said was, "Are you upset about Adrian leaving our table and dancing with that lady that has been flirting with him."

I looked at her and I couldn't lie. I felt like I could trust her. I said, "Yes I am, and I am not sure why I got upset to this degree."

She said, "Well, I know why. He's your husband. If it were my husband doing that I would be upset. I'm really surprised at him."

"Yeah, I guess you're right," I said. I couldn't explain to her why I didn't have a right to be upset.

She said, "Come on Charlotte, let's get out of here and you go get your man."

I laughed and said, "Right."

As we walked back into the dance, Adrian's eyes examined me and I walked up to him and said, "I think the next dance is mine." I raised my eyebrows as if this was a question.

He said, "I think you're right. I think it is." He looked at Annette and said, "Nice talking to you. I am going to dance with my wife."

When we were on the floor, he asked, "Are you okay?"

"Why do you asked?"

"The way you and Delores left the room. I could see something was wrong with you. I was worried."

"Really?"

"Yes. You looked stiff as a board. I was waiting to see if Ray would go out to check on you," he continued. "However, he never left the room."

"What," I exclaimed. "What are you talking about? Are you kidding me?"

He said, "No, I'm not kidding you. I thought he would go and check on his love."

"What gives you that idea?"

"Well, you left and didn't come back before. Well, you came back, but after a long talk with him outside in the hall. After Delores came back alone, I went to look for you and saw you and him having an intimate conversation."

By this time, the dance had come to an end and we are on our way to our seat. I didn't want to continue this conversation at the table with Herb and Delores, so I said, "We will talk about this at home. I think I might get too emotional in public, so let's discuss what you think you saw at home."

"All right," he answered.

After our discussion on the dance floor, I was in a much better mood. Adrian had misread what he saw and had retaliated by going over to Annette's table. Now that I knew that, I felt better and began to enjoy myself again. We shared jokes at the table and danced some more. I danced once with Herb and three more times with Adrian and then the dance was over. As we made our way out of the building, Annette tried to make eye contact with Adrian. I stepped in front of him and caused her eyes to meet mine. I gave her an unwavering stare to telepathically inform her that this man was mine. She rolled her eyes backward in her head and went on to her car. I didn't know what she expected to happen after the dance, but I sure intended to find out when we had our "talk" later on tonight.

When we reached our car, Adrian opened my door and by accident, his arm brushed my hand, and I felt a rush of desire. I jumped. My mind raced as I thought about the conversation we would have when we got home.

CHAPTER 21

We didn't speak on the way home, but I could sense the nearness of a storm that had been brewing for a long time. At home, I stepped out of my shoes and brought them to my bedroom. Adrian followed me there and stood in the doorway. I turned around and sat on the bed.

He said, "May I enter your bedroom?"

"Yes," I said, very much aware of what else I might have invited in.

"Well, tell me about the conversation with Ray." He continued to stand in the doorway. His eyes never left my face.

I said, "He told me he loved me and he was going to leave his wife if I would tell him to."

"What? So, in other words, he wanted to put the decision on you. Any guilt he would have, he could transfer to you. What an honorable fella? What did you say?"

I said emphatically, "I said no. I don't want him to leave his wife and kids."

"You did?"

"Yes, I did."

"What else did y'all say. Because y'all talked a good while and were completely absorbed with each other, when I saw y'all in the hall."

"I told him I did not want to be with him. I did not love him and any discussion we would have concerning Luke would have to include you."

"You said that?" he asked. I could see the tension leave his body. However, he still looked at me suspiciously.

"Yes, I said that. I said that several times. I wanted to make sure he understood any part he played in my life was going to be because of Luke and any part he played in Luke's life would be determined by all of us, including you."

He walked into the room and sat on the bed and took me into his arms. We just sat for a moment. I think he waited for me to pull away, but I didn't. In fact, I laid my head on his shoulder and it felt so good. I felt his arm tighten around me. Then I asked him, "Now, it's your turn, tell me about Annette?"

For a moment, he seemed surprised. "I almost said Annette who? But you're talking about me dancing with her and talking to her."

I said, "Yes, I am."

"I only did that after I saw you outside talking to Ray. You all seemed to be oblivious about anyone else. You didn't even see me standing in the doorway looking at you. It upset me and I wanted to upset you. I know that was childish, but I have feelings too. I'm sorry I did that. I should not have assumed anything when I saw you two talking. I guess it was my sense of insecurity."

"I'm sorry for what you think you saw," I said. "I had no control over that situation and I was handling it the best way I knew how. However, you did have control over your situation and in fact, you instigated it. But, I forgive you."

"What was that move you pulled on Annette when we were

leaving. For a moment, I thought that you were going to hit her. Look at Char, staking claim over her 'man'." He chuckled at first and then broke out into a laugh.

"Oh so you think that's funny, huh?"

"A little bit. I was a little surprised, but pleased that you thought you might lose me and decided that you weren't going to let it happen."

"Was she expecting to talk to you after the dance? That's what I thought. The way she was looking at you."

He continued to smile, as though I amused him to no end. "No, we had no plans for after the dance. Whatever her plans were, they were not discussed with me. I promise you that," he said.

Our eyes me and he got serious. "I'm sorry if I hurt you, Charlotte," he said. "I'm very sorry."

Then Adrian got really quiet, as if he was trying to decide if he was going to tell me something or not. "Char, I am going to tell you something I think you are old enough to be able to handle. Especially, since you not only processed the news about your father, but gave support to your sisters and your mother. I think it best to put everything out there, so you can handle it all at one time."

Oh my Lord, what is he about to tell me now? I thought. My heart rate accelerated again. Was there another woman he was interested in?

"The other day, you were asking me a lot of questions."

"Questions? Questions about what?"

"Well, you mentioned you thought you looked different from your family."

"Yes. I did," I said. My heart continued to pound.

"You also wondered why your mother and I are so close." He paused for a moment and then continued. "I talked with her yesterday, before she went to New Orleans and got her permission to tell you something. She really did not want to ever tell you this, but I feel it may give you some answers to some questions that are bothering you. Since you now know about your father, this should clear some other things up."

I sat in stunned silence. I'd wanted answers, but in the last few weeks, answers had come at me left and right. I didn't know if I could handle anything else and remain sane.

Adrian stopped and observed me as if to gauge whether he should continue. "I was nineteen years old and walking down Perret's Path through the woods. I was taking the short cut to get to the highway when I heard someone moaning. I stopped and looked around and saw your mother curled up in a ball under some bushes a few feet off of the path. Her clothes were torn and she was bloody around the mouth. Her face was swollen and one of her eyes were swollen shut. She was crying something awful." I stared a hole through him so hard that he stopped again and asked me, "You okay?"

"Yes, I'm okay." I said, not quite sure how I felt. Besides being frightened about what he was about to tell me, now I also felt empathy for my mother.

"I ran to her to see how I could help. At first she didn't want me around. Didn't want me to see her that way. We didn't know each other well at that time. Even though she told me to go away, I didn't leave, because I knew she needed help. Finally, she allowed me to take her home. She put her arm around my neck, and I put my arm around her waist, and supported her until we reached her house. Which was about one hundred yards away through the woods. On the way, she told me what had happened to her. She had been attacked by one of her husband's cousins. She had been raped and because she had resisted, she had been beaten."

As I listened to the story, tears rolled down my cheeks.

"When we finally got to her back door, Lucien opened it. He

was shocked when he saw her and wanted to start a fight with me. He thought I had done it. When we got him settled down and then got her settled down, she told him what had happened. He was so angry. He got his shotgun and wanted to go shoot his cousin. I talked him out of it. He didn't need to go to jail. He had a wife and his little girl, Laura, to take care of."

My body tensed up when I heard what he'd said. Only Laura was born yet.

"I told him I would go with him to see his cousin and make sure it was a fair fight. I walked down the road and got your Aunt Rae to come over and tend to your mother. Me and your daddy walked the two miles to his cousin's house, and he whipped him good. I was there to make sure none of his brothers tried to jump in and double-team your daddy. I don't think they were going to anyway, after they found out what their brother had done. Anyway, I walked with Luke back home afterwards and cleaned up his wounds. It had been a hard fought battle and he had some scars to prove it."

He took my hand in his and continued. "We became the best of friends after that, the three of us." Then he paused. "Sweetheart ... nine months later, you were born."

He stretched out his arms to me and I entered them and felt the pressure of his embrace as he squeezed me tightly. I was in shock. Did he just tell me that my father was not my father? The man who had played with me, had tossed me around in the air, whom I missed so much when he left, whom I still worried about, the man I am mad as hell at right now. You mean, that man is not my father?

"I have always felt very protective of you and Feen ever since. Feen and I have had a bond. It has evolved over the years and thanks to you, our bond is even stronger now, just different. But I want you to believe that Luke loved you. From the day, you were born and he held you in his arms, you were his daughter. I was there and you can't fake that. He never thought of you as anything else. I want you to know that and I want you to believe that."

"You know, that's why I thought he left?" I cried. "I believed he left because of me. In my child's mind, I thought it was something I had done. Now when I finally know the reason he left, I find out that he's not my father. That I am the product of a rape. The reason I am here is because some sick person decided to beat and rape my mother. God, how much more of this am I expected to endure," I asked rhetorically. "Who all know Mom was raped?"

"Besides Luke, Feen, Rae and Luke's cousin who raped her and his brothers, I don't think anyone else know. Feen never told anyone else but her sister and she's sworn to silence. The rapist and his brothers didn't tell anyone. They don't want anyone to know they would do something like that."

"Notice I did not tell you his name. I don't think you are ready for that yet. When you are and you want to know his name, I will tell you. Okay?"

He was right. I didn't want to know his name. Right now I was too angry with him. As far as I was concerned, Lucien Ford was my father. No matter how mad at him I was.

"How do you feel?" Adrian asked.

"A whole range of feelings. All of the revelations I'm digesting. My whole world is different than I thought it was. I am not who I thought I was."

"Oh, yes you are. You're the same person Luke and Feen love, who fought her way to get an education and become a teacher. You're the same girl who looks out for her sisters and who is a wonderful mother to Lil Luke. Don't you forget that."

"Now, I understand my mother better. I understand some of the warnings she's always giving me, and the sadness in her eyes behind the laughter. I love her even more than before, if that's possible. All of the suffering she went through to have me and the sorrow she is going through right now."

"You have her spirit. There was something that kept drawing me to her home and you girls after Luke left. People kept telling me I was sweet on her. I didn't know if I was or not, but I knew there was a strong something that made me feel I was needed there. But, as close as we were, and I mean we were close, 'specially after Luke left, I never crossed that line of intimacy. Something held me back, but I never suspected my destiny lay in you. God put me there when you were conceived and I've felt the overpowering urge to keep protecting you ever since. You are my destiny, Princess. I love you."

"Really?" I said. "Do you really?"

"I do really. You are a gorgeous and remarkable lady."

"In what way do you love me," I asked.

"This way," he whispered.

He took my chin in his hand and lifted my head from his shoulders and kissed me on each side of my neck. Then he kissed me all over my chest, the part that was exposed through my dress. He came back up to my neck again and then kissed my chin, each cheek, my forehead, my nose, my eyes and finally my lips very softly. By the time, he got to my lips, I was so ready to kiss him. He kissed me with long deep kisses. Kisses that seemed like he wanted to catch up for all of those months we hadn't touched each other. Kisses that stirred up feelings way down deep within me and that begin to salve the wounds of my heart, and the hurt I'd just endured through the knowledge of the events that surrounded my birth. I removed my clothes and he removed his. He laid me on the bed and kissed each breast and I moaned. He said, "Now, I can call you my chocolate princess. Princess, I love you."

"Adrian, I love you." I knew it was true. I don't know when it happened, but it was in full bloom. I loved this darling man with all of my heart and soul.

We made love. As I reveled in this feeling of passion and abandonment, I knew I wanted to be this way with him forever. As we moaned and continued to make love, I felt something start from my feet and run the length of my back and then to the center of me. The sensations were overwhelming and I felt my body convulse and then go still.

We lay in each other's arms and he whispered again, "Oh, my sweet Princess, I love you."

"I love you too," I said.

I lay on my side and touched him lightly on his chest as he lay on his back. "When did you start to fall in love with me?"

"I'm not sure when it started, but I started to realize it at Christmas, when Eric was here and you called me Husband. It kind of surprised me that you thought of me that way, when we hadn't been together as husband and wife. I knew then I wanted to be your husband. I love the way you were kind to Eric, the pleasure of your scent in the morning when you whiz by me on your way out the door, the way your eyes broaden when you're uncertain about a situation, the smoothness and rich color of your skin and how it looks next to mine, how you lean into me whenever we're sitting together, how you take care of Luke and the way you take care of me." He pulled me close to him and I laid my head on his chest.

"When did you realize it?" he asked.

"I think I've always loved you. When I felt like I was falling in love with you was soon after we were married. At the Bouchérie, when you sang to me. Miss Sara hit the nail right on the head when she said, 'That chile gonna faint just lookin' at 'em.'"

He laughed. "Really? I had no idea. I'm gonna have to make sure I sing to you."

"It's going to take me a while to digest the bombshell you just told me. Who I am, my relationship with my daddy, Lucien and the man whose sperm created me."

"I know, Princess. It's going to be hard but you can get through this. You are the same person today you were yesterday. Whether your biological Daddy is Lucien or somebody else, you're the same person."

"I know what you're saying. I know I am going to want to know who this guy is who attacked Mom. I don't want to deal with it today or next week. Tonight, I am enjoying the comfort of my husband's arms. My husband's arms. Doesn't that sound delicious?" I said, giving him a light peck on the lips.

"Yes, it does."

"I want to take that in completely and when I'm ready, I will ask you to tell me the name."

"Sounds good to me," he said. "On another subject, I guess I will clean out my apartment in Houston. I kept it for my return after the divorce, but since there isn't going to be a divorce, it's time for me to let it go. I guess I'm assuming things. We are not getting a divorce. Right?" he asked.

"No Baby," I answered. "We are not getting a divorce."

He sat up in bed and pulled me up to a sitting position. Turning me to face him, he took my hand in his and then took my wedding ring off. He placed the ring back on my finger, and said, "With this ring, I take you as my wife, until death do us part, with all the rights and responsibilities being married brings. I will love you and honor you and keep you safe to the best of my ability." Then he leaned over and kissed me lightly on the mouth.

I then took his hand, took his wedding band off and then placed it back on his finger and said, "With this ring, I take you as my husband, until death do us part. I will cherish you, love you, honor you and support you in your endeavors to provide and protect our family, until death do us part." I kissed him on the lips and then kissed him again and again and again...

In the afterglow of the consummation of our marriage, I prepared myself for sleep after a day filled with family turmoil, merriment, and revelations, both heart wrenching and heart-warming. I thought of that day, almost two years ago, at Keykey's funeral. When I'd felt the wind knocked out of me and the agony of her loss had blocked my vision. I'd longed for her and to be cherished by someone like she had been. She had felt so loved by Blain because he allowed her to sleep on his chest all night long, despite his own discomfort. Well, Keykey, I've found him. He had been there all along. He had nurtured and protected me for as long as I could remember. I took a deep breath and let the anxieties of the day evaporate and invite in visions of a sweet and supportive relationship. I laid my head on Adrian's chest and with his arms around me, I slept there all night long.

THE END

SUGGESTED QUESTIONS SUITABLE FOR BOOK CLUB GROUPS

1. Why did Keykey's death impact Charlotte so strongly?

2. Describe the relationship between Charlotte and her mother? Why did she feel lighter after she'd told her mother that she was pregnant?

3. Describe the relationship between Adrian and Feen? How do you think Feen really felt about the wedding?

4. Do you believe in hoodoo? Why or why not?

5. What was the first time you noticed Charlotte being concerned about her identity?

6. What kind of person was Ray Dean? What are some of his character flaws? What are some of his virtues?

7. What kind of person was Adrian Fonteneau? What are some of his character flaws? What are some of his virtues?

8. Do teachers still have morals clauses in their contracts now? Do you think they should have them? Why or why not?

9. Was Laura correct in leaving Rick? Should she have done it sooner? Why?

10. Which suitor would you have chosen for Charlotte, Adrian or Ray? Why?

11. What were some of Charlotte's insecurities? What were the reasons that caused these anxieties?

12. How is life different now socially, economically and educationally than they were in the 1960s?

13. Do you think that Lucien was happy with the decision he'd made many years ago? Why or why not?

14. Do you agree with Charlotte's concern about the age differences of her mother and Blain when she wasn't concerned about the age differences between her and Adrian? Why or Why not?

ABOUT THE AUTHOR

Susane was born and reared near Red River in Marksville, Louisiana. Playing along the banks and levees of the river allowed her imagination to soar. Susane's writing exhibits her love for her childhood home as well as the turmoil and dissension that were a part of life in the 1960s South.

She earned a B. S. degree in Accounting and Teacher Certification in Business Courses from Northwestern State University, Natchitoches, Louisiana.

She has worked in the telecommunications industry, sold real estate, taught high school and owned small businesses.

The mother of three children and five grandchildren, she is an avid genealogist. She lives with her fur baby, a poodle named Gail, in Texas. She is currently working on her next novel.

Made in the USA
San Bernardino, CA
06 January 2018